GODS

OF

ANOTHER

KIND

A NOVEL

STEVEN DECKER

Quotes of scripture are from the World English Bible.

ISBN 979-8-9889262-1-4 (print)
ISBN 979-8-9889262-0-7(eBook)

Library of Congress Control Number: 2023914828

Cover design by Damonza
Interior design and formatting by Sabrina Milazzo, www.sabrinamilazzo.net

First edition 2023

Visit the author's website at www.stevendecker.com
Published by TIER Books LLC

For the family

Novels by Steven Decker

Distant Finish

The Time Chain Series:
    Time Chain
    The Balance of Time
    Addicted to Time

The Another Kind Series:
    Child of Another Kind
    Earth of Another Kind
    Gods of Another Kind

Walking Into Dreams

PART ONE

Chapter 1

T he woods were lovely the morning my life changed. Dark and deep. Still and quiet. Packed with soaring maples and beech and speckled with thickets of hemlock. The foliage above me was so dense that it blocked the light of incipient dawn, blanketing me with night.

My dogs scampered off the trail. The beagle's nose was pressed to the ground, on vacuum cleaner mode (which very much reminded me of the sound of a pig snorting), leading the pack after some unknown animal scent, no doubt fresh. The white tip of his tail pointed toward heaven. I peered through the tightly-spaced trees and caught the black outline of the range of mountains to the East, wondering if I'd be treated to a rare glimpse of the sun rising over their summit. Too early, but soon. No matter. I didn't need Sol's help to navigate this familiar trail.

The dogs and I walked here every morning, all year long, and in the evenings after our dinner. My property sits adjacent to this forest, technically a public space, but I rarely saw anyone out here. Most hikers preferred the routes which took them from hut to hut, where they could get food and spend the night, and there were also the fast walkers loping down the Appalachian Trail, which passed by not far away. But here, where I lived, was a pristine slice of nature that included a clear mountain lake on the other side, which I would soon reach if I followed my present course.

I turned right and wound deeper into my semi-private sanctuary, my footfalls barely registering a sound the human ear could detect. Still, I heard the dogs tramping nearby, enjoying themselves but never far from my side. They believed I'd be safer if they stayed with me. And it was undoubtedly true that a lone bear or a pack of coyotes, the rare bobcat, would be more afraid of a bunch of primarily large dogs than they would of me. But it didn't matter. I'd survived here in the White Mountains of New Hampshire for thirty years, scraping out a living through my writing, a solitary pursuit for a solitary man. Save for the dogs and Jack the cat, I was alone.

The light of day greeted me as I emerged from the forest onto the shores of the lake. The cheerful music of birds waking filled the air as I approached the water, and I thought I heard splashing. What could it be? A fish bursting through the surface and plunging back into the depths? A family of otters playing joyfully in the place they called home? But then I saw something that took my breath away. A young woman washing herself gently in the cold mountain lake, her clothes and towel lying in a haphazard pile on the shore. When I first saw her, all that was visible were her head, graceful neck, and a trace of glistening bare shoulders. But then she stood up.

She was tall, with an angular face, a strong chin, and high cheekbones. Her body was firm and looked strong. She was one of the most beautiful creatures I'd ever seen, and she was very pregnant. Her swollen belly pressed hard against the skin of her abdomen, looking like an over-inflated flesh-colored beach ball about to explode. And there was something else about her that made her unique: she was completely bald. I was close enough to ascertain that she had no hair on her entire body. Not even eyebrows or eyelashes. I could see the goosebumps covering her skin, so as you can imagine, nothing was left to the imagination. I tried to do the gentlemanly thing and turn away. It was difficult. And then her saucer-like blue eyes spotted me, and I was caught, unable to move.

The dogs had come out of the underbrush and gathered around me, peering at the woman as intensely as I was but making no sound other than the panting of their breaths. I was at a loss for words and felt clumsy and old, ugly in the face of such glorious beauty, but then words from a female voice came into my mind. *It's all right.* She gazed at me for an eternity of about five seconds but made no move to go to her clothes. Instead, she smiled and turned away from me, her belly disappearing in front of her, and I couldn't help but bear witness to the curves of her body, so perfect, so wonderful, so foreign to a man who hadn't been with a woman for more years than I could remember.

She moved out into the lake, and her hands came over her head and joined together, forming an arch. Then she rose high into the air, her entire body leaving the water, and she plunged delicately back down into the chilly lake, producing a tiny splash and disappearing from my sight. The ripples edged outward, the only remaining signs of her presence other than her abandoned clothes on the shore.

I waited for her to reappear, but she didn't, not for a long time. And then I saw her head pop up, far in the distance, too far for a person to have swum underwater, at least two hundred meters from the shore. I watched as she turned back to look for me, and then her arm came up, and she waved. At me? My heart quickened, and I wondered why she had done that.

Continuing her swim above the water this time and using the freestyle stroke, she seemed to be pulling toward the opposite shore. After several moments, she emerged from the water and stepped onto the land on the far side. The distance was so great I could barely see her, but she was definitely standing there, undoubtedly dripping wet and cold, with no towel or clothes because they were here, on this side.

She waved again, turned, and walked into the forest, gone from my sight. I stood listlessly beside the lake, a bewildered and lonely man who wasn't sure what he'd just seen. And then, a thought came to the forefront of my mind that must have been waiting in line since I first encountered the young woman. I knew who she was.

Chapter 2

My name is Zachary Hurts. I wish I could tell you my friends call me Zach, but the only friends I have don't speak Human. I'm fifty-two years old and have been living alone up here in the woods since I was twenty-one. My hair is long and straight. Light brown with hints of gray in it now, and I usually tie it back in a ponytail. How did I come to live alone out here, you ask? It's not a long story, and I'm sure we'll get to it at some point, but it doesn't matter right now. For now, suffice it to say that I love animals, and this is a great place to be among them. But I was telling you about the woman I saw in the lake, and I'd like to continue that story if you don't mind because it didn't end there, not by a long stretch.

On the other hand, it would be impolite not to introduce you to my family by going straight to the good stuff. Don't worry, this book isn't about dogs and cats, but I loved them more than anything until I met Gwen, and they deserve at least to be mentioned.

The beagle's name is Wilson, and he's the pack leader, even though he's the smallest of the nine. Wilson does what he wants, and that usually involves following his nose wherever it leads him. The others seem to know he picks up more scents, and they've gotten a bit lazy over the years regarding their noses, relying instead on the unrelenting sniffing of Brother Wilson.

Jenny is a black lab mixed with something predatory, like a Doberman. She loves people but hates other dogs, except for her family. Jenny's the oldest of the crew. Thirteen now and slowing down, but she'll still attack any animal that isn't us. She continues to eat and walk, and that covers a lot of what dogs do. And she barks at whatever she sees, although her hearing is questionable at this point. We get a lot of barking for the sake of barking from Jenny. To prove she can still do it, I guess.

Gus is a yellow lab mixed with some kind of long and lanky dog, maybe a Great Dane. He's tall and lean but still tips the scales at about 120 pounds. A gentle giant is the best way to capture the essence of Gus. He goes with the flow but would submit to the will of a chipmunk if it came down to it.

Tank is a Griffin mix, meaning he has a beard. He's got relatively long hair, black mixed with white, and is the filthiest dog I've ever had. Can't get enough mud, so I have a dog shower outside that I use on him whenever he's been wallowing.

Daisy is some kind of border collie-shepherd mix that came to us one day out of the woods. She'd been living in the wild for a while when she became part of the pack, but I wouldn't call her a wild dog. Loyal is what I'd call her. Appreciative. We'd seen her hanging out by the lake for a few weeks, and one day she followed us home. The others got all macho with her, but she quickly put them in their place so nobody messes with her anymore.

Nicky is a quiet old Newfoundland mix with long hair, but he's the best hunter of the bunch. Too good, really. It brings an ache to my heart when I see some of the things he brings home. I won't go into it, though. Just know that I'm not a hunter. I love all the animals, and I hate to see one taken down by a dog with access to two squares a day. But I love him too, so I put up with it.

Milo is a runt from the streets of Puerto Rico that was dropped off at my vet anonymously. They called to see if I could fit another one into the pack, and of course, I said yes. He's a short-haired brown dog with the head of a pit bull but the curly tail of a chihuahua, and believe it or not, the vet said he had both of those in him, plus a dozen other breeds, according to the DNA testing. But he's a sweetheart. A little needy, though, for human contact, and I'm spread pretty thin. Keeping them fed and watered takes up much of my free time.

Molly is one of three purebreds in the bunch. A golden retriever, distinguished from most of that breed by her beefy physique. To say it politely, Molly is overweight by a mile. But she hangs with the pack in every circumstance, and that's all that matters.

Mac is a golden doodle but looks more like a white sheepdog because I don't trim his hair enough. He's a service dog dropout that couldn't make the cut because he was afraid of everything. But it didn't take long for the pack to teach him how to be a dog, and now he might be the happiest of the group. But don't send him out on an errand without his buddies!

Now that I've gone over the list, I won't fawn over my dogs for the rest of the book because that's not what this is all about. You might wonder, however, what would happen to them if something happened to me, and I've got that covered. I told them I'd left a note on the side table beside my bed. The message said, "Something happened to our owner. Please help." If that unfortunate circumstance occurred, the dogs were to grab the note, hustle out through the dog door, and run down to the vet's office. I even had them do a practice run, like a fire drill. I told them it was just practice and they didn't have to go all the way into the vet's office or give him the note. I just wanted to see if they would actually take the note and go there. I counted to three and said, "Go."

Wilson was the first to get to my bedside table, although Daisy and Milo were right on his heels. The rest were either uninterested or didn't quite understand what was happening. Wilson reared up, put his front paws on the table, took the note in his mouth, and rushed out of the house through the dog door. Daisy and Milo went out right after him, and then the rest of them realized something was going on and dashed after them. There was a log jam at the dog door, but all of them eventually made it through. I ran outside and saw the three leaders waiting for the others, and then the pack took off down my gravel driveway. I told myself I needed to see this, so I jumped in my old Jeep, grabbed the keys off the floorboard, and headed down the long gravel driveway.

I got to the end of the driveway and looked left. They were already near the top of the rise and well on their way. Nine dogs running down the country lane, going to town. They returned around thirty minutes later, huffing and puffing and lining up at the drinking trough like horses after the Kentucky Derby. I told them great job, and felt much better about things, except I got a call from the vet a few minutes later inquiring about my well-being. Apparently, the pack had dropped the note on the floor in the reception area and then hauled butt out of there. My vet was an old guy named Jim Mason who'd seen a lot of things in his long career in town but never anything like that. I explained everything to him, and he was impressed and glad I was okay. And it was good that he knew about my plan anyway.

Oh, and I forgot to mention, I've got a cat too. One-eyed Jack. He's there to hunt mice but isn't very good at it. He's an undersized tabby, big enough to kill a mouse, but with only one eye. Maybe he just can't see them. The dogs all love him, and vice versa, but he mainly hangs out inside, except when he has to go to the little boys' room. Everyone except me does that outside, including Jack.

Now back to the matter we started with. A few months passed, and there was no sign of the woman. I'd incorporated the lake into our daily walking regimen since that morning I was telling you about. Several routes don't go by the lake, but we haven't taken those since the sighting of the woman. At first, my excuse was to check and see if her clothes were still there, and the answer was yes. After a few days, I decided to pick them up and bring them home. I washed and folded them and put them on a little table I don't use much in the corner of the living room. Was I expecting her to come looking for them? Well, "expecting" is too strong of a word to describe my feelings on that subject. "Hoping" would be the more appropriate choice.

I told you I knew who she was, and I did because she was famous, probably the most renowned alien of all time because of the things she'd done. She was known everywhere on Earth after she stood up on that stage with President Marks back in 2029, when they announced to the world that the aliens had been helping us and living here for a long time.

The lady in my lake was named Madison Pace, but everyone called her Maddie; at least, the tabloids did. She seemed like a decent sort of being to hear her talk, but then she murdered the President of Russia, who was supposedly an alien himself, and disappeared. Many people were upset about that, but they played this tape on the television that allegedly was the meeting between her and Sidorov when she killed him, and he didn't sound like the kind of person you'd want at the head of a nuclear power. Still, some hated her and probably would have tried to kill her if she stuck around, but she's gone. Her replacement is a bald-headed guy, I can't remember his name, but he's got eyebrows and eyelashes, so I don't know why she doesn't.

By the way, this whole group from outer space nearly tanked my career. I used to write science fiction, but I switched to fantasy after the aliens were announced. I mean, why write sci-fi when you've got the most powerful beings in the universe living on some giant space station that's supposedly right here in the solar system? Nobody's seen it, but people visit it, and some have even gone to live there, so it's pretty much a fact that writing sci-fi is a dead-end street these days. People live in a sci-fi world now, so they don't need or want to read pretend stories about it.

That's my take, anyway. Some of the big names have carried on with science fiction, but that's not me. I was never a big name, but now that I've met the most famous alien in the world, maybe I will be. Oops, I wasn't supposed to tell you I met her. Soon though, I promise.

Several months passed, and I never saw Madison Pace swimming in my lake again. I didn't know why she'd been there to begin with, why she left her clothes, or why she didn't return. But I wanted to know. And I wanted to find out if she'd had her baby and if everything was okay. And if I'm honest, I yearned to just meet her, maybe talk for a few minutes, because I found her story so intriguing. I figured that if I'd gotten so close to her, and she had sent me a thought message (three words, but hey, it was something!), even waved at me, I kind of deserved to meet her. So I continued to take the trail that passed by the lake through the summer and into the fall. Never saw her. Then one day in early October, we had just returned to the house from the morning walk. And there was a knock at my door.

Chapter 3

Yes, it was her. I opened the door, and there she was, smiling at me as if I were an old friend. She was noticeably thinner than the last time I'd seen her, and she was wearing clothes; a dark green flannel shirt and faded jeans, hiking boots on her feet. Her head was still bald, and the eyebrows and eyelashes were still missing, leading me to conclude that this was a permanent condition. But it didn't matter. She was here! And she was staring at me with those enormous blue eyes. I was flustered but had to say something.

"Good morning," I said. "Are you lost?" Of course, I was trying to pretend I didn't know her and had never seen her before, to no avail.

"Hi, Zachary!" she said. "I hope I'm not disturbing you, but I was wondering if we could chat for a moment."

I felt my eyebrows go up, but I tried to remain calm and collected.

"Of course. And your name is?"

"Maddie Pace. But you know that already."

I shuffled backward to make room for her to enter the house, and she stepped up off the porch and into my living room. She was slightly taller than me, but I was barefoot, and she had on hiking boots, so I figured we were about the same height. I'm six feet one inch tall, so I surmised she was too.

"May I offer you tea or coffee?" I asked.

"Coffee would be great!" she said.

"Come on into the kitchen. We can sit at the table there. Oh, and I've got your clothes!"

"Yes, I know," she said, following me into the kitchen.

"I apologize for the state of things. I haven't done the morning vacuuming." This was true, but I swear to you that I vacuum at least once a day.

"I imagine nine dogs keep you pretty busy," she said.

"Yeah, but the cat's no trouble." I was trying my best to be funny. Casual, you know. Not the way I was feeling, however. I was nervous. My heart was fluttering on overdrive. I rarely see people, and here was one of the most famous people on Earth, right in my home. "Please, Maddie, have a seat over there at the table, and I'll get the coffee. How do you like it?"

"Black is fine," she said.

"A person of my own heart!" I said, turning to reach for two cups.

"More than you would know," she said.

I didn't turn back to her when she said this, but it did throw me for a loop. I remember rumors of her and her kind being mind readers, and that was proving to be the case. And she could speak using telepathy. I'd learned that back in June. But I wondered how I was like her, other than both of us enjoying our coffee black. Well, she was here for a reason, so maybe I would get the answer to that question soon. I brought the cups to the table, set them down, and sat around the corner from her. The table was square, hand-made from the maple that grew in woods like these by a craftsman in town.

"So you had the baby?" I asked. "Everything go okay?" I mean, there were no secrets between us, so why continue with the ruse that I didn't know her and had never seen her before?

"Twins!" she said. "A boy and a girl."

"Awesome! What are their names?"

"The girl is Casey, and the boy is Tony."

"Are you married?" I asked.

"No," she said. "But Gino and I might as well be married."

"Where is he, by the way?"

"He's on Earth Station. That's where we live."

"Why are you here, Maddie?"

She smiled, took a sip of coffee, and then put her cup down. "I want to talk to you."

"About?"

"About you."

"Not much to tell there," I said, confused and uncertain about where this was going. "I live alone here with my dogs and cat and write books for a living. That's pretty much the whole story."

She was still smiling, staring at me with those incredible blue eyes. It was intimidating. "I'm here to add to that story, Zachary."

"How so?"

"Did you ever wonder how you can communicate with animals?" she asked.

Hmmm. I never talked about that with anyone, but if she was reading my mind, she would know. But did she know that was the reason I had moved up here in the first place, thirty-one years ago?

"Yes, I know that," she said. "It was your parents' vacation home, and they gave you permission to live here when you were twenty-one. When they passed, you inherited it. And I know a lot more than that, too. You were born in 1986, for example. Did you know that was the same year I was born?"

"I did not," I said. "And since you look to be only around thirty years old, I would say you either have excellent genes and a great workout plan, or else it ain't true!" I smiled to lighten the mood, and she smiled back.

"It's kind of the former," she said. "The genes. But we can talk about that later. I want to ask you if you know where you were born, Zachary?"

"Why yes, of course. I was born over in Littleton. It's about thirty miles from here."

"Hmmm," she mused. "How do I break this to you?"

"What?" I asked. I had my hands around my coffee cup as it sat on the table, and I realized I was squeezing it very hard.

"I know your parents were in their late forties when you came along, Zachary. Did you ever wonder how your mom could have had you at such a ripe old age? It isn't completely unheard of, but back in 1986, it wasn't at all common. Still isn't."

Of course, I had wondered. But I chose not to ask them. They were good parents. And they were my parents!

"They were indeed your parents, Zachary. But just like me, you were adopted. They just never bothered to tell you. After all, you were only two months old when they took you in, and they made a decision, as some parents of adopted children do, not to tell you."

I'm sure she was right. I have a vague memory from when I was five years old of thinking that very thing. You see, back when I was very young, I could look at someone and know their memories, and that was a memory I gathered from them. But then something happened, and I couldn't do that anymore. Instead, I could hear the thoughts of animals and send thoughts to them. I was too young to consider the why of any of it, and I never thought about it after that. But I also never told anyone about my abilities with animals. Not even my parents. But now that Maddie was there, telling me I was adopted, it wasn't really news to me. Old news, really.

"You were struck by lightning when you were five, right?" she asked.

No secrets, indeed. Not with this one. "Yes," I said. "But I survived. It wasn't too bad. I've got some scars on my back, but that's the extent of it."

"The lightning is what changed your abilities," said Maddie. "At least, that's what I think happened. And I'm not sure if you care, but I can't communicate with animals. None of our kind can, except you."

"I'm not one of you," I said, somewhat indignantly. I knew who I was, or at least believed I knew. "I'm just a normal human being with one unique ability. I don't read minds like you, and I don't transport myself from place to place except with my own two legs or that Jeep outside."

"I feel the same way about myself," said Maddie.

"What do you mean?" I asked, upset and confused.

"That I'm human!" she said. "I was raised here on Earth too. And I'm from the same batch of Imprints that you're from. And while the Makers considered us a mistake, to me, I'm a miracle. Because I became human while I was here. And so did you. But there's a technicality, Zachary. Technically, we're not human."

"How can you prove that?" I asked.

"There are many ways," she said. "We can get you an MRI, and it will show that your brain is different, physically. But it would be better if you just listened to me. Let me tell you what I know, and you make up your own mind, okay?"

How could I refuse? "Are you hungry, Maddie? This is usually breakfast time for me."

Chapter 4

I made breakfast for both of us, and we continued to talk. Maddie didn't eat eggs and bacon, my go-to breakfast, but I had oatmeal and fruit, which she enjoyed very much. Speaking of enjoying, my dogs were fascinated with her. They gathered around in the kitchen like a group of children listening to a storyteller, sitting on their haunches, and behaving in a way I'd never seen before. They only stuck together as a group when we were in the woods, but there they were, hypnotized by her presence.

"Your dogs are pretty cool," she said. "They're so well-behaved, and each one is so different from the next."

"This isn't normal for them. Most mornings, after the walk, a few go upstairs to bed, and the rest go outside to guard. Jenny stays with me."

My house was a two-story box with a roof, with three bedrooms and a bath upstairs and one bedroom and bath on the main floor. It was a frame house covered in long plank cedar siding stained brown with a steep green shingled roof. The floors inside were all maple, and even though it was a tough wood, the tramping of the dogs wore it out every ten years or so, and I would have it replaced. That wasn't as expensive as you might think since there were a lot of flooring manufacturers up here, and they always had rejects I could pick up for a lot less than the regular price. Plus, I'd laid out area rugs to help preserve the floor and because it was more comfortable for the dogs. Their dog beds were all in the upstairs bedrooms, except for Jenny's. She had a dog bed at the foot of mine. Since she'd lost her hearing, Jenny wanted to stay within my sight, and she was the oldest. I always favored the oldest.

"Well, they're great," said Maddie. "I've never been around animals on Earth or Earth Station. Actually, we don't have any land animals on Earth Station, and I'd like to change that. We're continuously working to make it a better place to live. If I can't live on Earth, then I want my home to be the best version of Earth it can be."

"Why can't you live here anymore, Maddie?"

She scrunched her mouth up in the way people do when they're frustrated. "You know, the whole Sidorov thing."

"I don't think a majority hold that against you, Maddie. After they played that tape of your meeting with him, most people felt your actions were fully justified."

"Most people," she said, frowning. "But the politicians still harp about international law and murder and want me in jail."

"But the people are with you, Maddie. You need to know that. I've read up on it a lot since I saw you a few months back."

"Yeah," she said. "But hey, let's talk about you. About why I'm here and how I found you."

Maddie explained the history of Imprints on Earth and how she and I were an experimental "model" that didn't know who they were until they reached puberty. We were here to "mark" humans as either empathic or narcissistic; some of those ended up reborn on Earth Station and had the chance to become Makers. All of us could read people's pasts and even send thoughts into people's minds. Apparently, I lost the ability to do that when I was struck by lightning. After that, I could get into the heads of most animals but not into the heads of humans.

"How did you find me?" I asked.

"My abilities were enhanced when I was awarded the assignment to deal with Sidorov. Part of that was the ability to find Imprints on Earth and use them as beacons to travel here. After I retired, from time to time, I made secret visits to Earth because I enjoy it here very much. I had heard about the White Mountains of New Hampshire and love to hike, but no Imprints were showing on our map up there. The Teacher said there used to be one here, but he had died. I think he was talking about you. Anyway, I don't need a map to find Imprints. I can feel their presence from great distances. I scanned this area and picked up a blip that turned out to be you."

I wasn't fighting it anymore. Maddie's case was too persuasive for me to deny the facts. I'd always been different; even after the lightning, I was still different. I loved reading and could read very quickly, so I had a vast amount of background knowledge about writing itself and many other subjects, and I decided to try writing myself. It took a while to find a publisher, but eventually, I found a small one and earned a little money. With the explosion of self-publishing, I had left my publisher and gone out on my own, learning that I could do as good a job of marketing as them and receive a much larger share of the earnings from the books. But that's another story.

"Why are you telling me all of this, Maddie? What's your purpose here?" I asked.

"I want you to come live on Earth Station," she said. "You and your dogs could help us make it a better place."

"The dogs are welcome there?" I asked. "What about my cat?"

"Yes, One-eyed Jack is very welcome. He would be the first cat to come there. And your dogs would be the first dogs."

"What about the other animals?" I asked. "The ones that live in the forest?"

You've learned that I can communicate with animals. Dogs, cats, deer, bears, coyotes, birds, even snakes. It wasn't speech communication, though. I could pick up their thoughts, rudimentary compared to a human, but they were still thoughts. And I could send my thoughts to them. It was essential to keep my communication on the same level as their ability to understand, but I'd gotten pretty good at that as the years passed.

"You mean the wild animals, right?" she asked.

"Yeah. They're kind of my family, too, you see."

"I'm not sure moving them would be easy," she said. "And do you think that's what they'd want anyway?"

"Probably not," I said. "But I'd miss them."

She squeezed her eyes together and paused for a few seconds. Then she said, "I have an idea!"

"What?"

"We'll make them!"

"You can do that?" I asked.

"Well, not me, but the Makers can do it. They made all the fish in the sea, so I don't see why they can't also make land animals. I can do scans of the ones you want to bring, and the Makers can take it from there."

"I don't know," I said, uncertainty bubbling in my gut. "I'm happy here. After all, this is the real deal. Earth Station is just a facsimile from what I'm hearing."

"True," she said. "But Earth Station has one thing Earth doesn't."

"What's that?"

"Everything that lives there is immortal."

Chapter 5

Spring 2039

Of course, I said yes. Eventually. Maddie returned several times, and we would take trips into the forest so she could get scans of the wild animals. I knew where they were instinctively, and I could tell them to hang tight and that the person with me was safe. The bobcats were a little wary, but the bears and coyotes lingered long enough for her to get the scans. They seemed intrigued by Maddie in the same way my dogs were. A few of them even nuzzled up to her to be petted. She loved it! And it was amazing, even more so because she'd never been around animals. Frankly, I was a little jealous, but even more pronounced was my desire to figure out why.

I asked her how the food chain would work on Earth Station. It seemed impossible to populate the wilderness with all the various kinds of wildlife, from the smallest ant up, so that all the animals would have the food they needed. Maddie suggested that if I didn't mind, they could make all the animals herbivores. I liked that idea and readily agreed to it.

Anyway, I finally decided to go in the spring of 2039. I rented my place to two technicians from Jim Mason's vet practice, telling them I'd be leaving the country and taking my animals with me. At that time, I didn't know if I'd be returning, but Maddie had promised me that if I wasn't happy on Earth Station, it would be no problem to return.

On the day we left, Maddie brought a tall man with long blond hair to help with the transfer. She introduced him as "Teacher," and it seemed he might be one of the head guys, the Makers, but she didn't mention that. Maddie had told me I didn't need to pack anything because they had everything we needed there. She'd even taken samples of my dog and cat food at one point and told me they would duplicate it up there and that it would be waiting for us. I stored all my clothes in the basement and was ready to go.

We all had to be touching to make the jump, so the three humans (or whatever we were) got in a circle, and I told the dogs to line up around us and shake. Jack was sitting on my shoulder as I had told him to, but when I leaned down, he dug in with his claws, and it hurt. The dogs all put up one of their paws, and our group of three made contact with them using both hands, spreading our fingers wide so we didn't miss any of them. I made contact with Maddie's thumb with my pinky, and I guess that was enough because suddenly, we blinked out of existence on Earth and materialized on Earth Station. I noticed Wilson, the beagle, was missing, which wasn't surprising since he tended to do what he wanted at all times and had probably missed out on the opportunity to travel to another world by failing to shake. But Maddie popped back to Earth and soon reappeared with fat Wilson in her arms.

"He's heavier than he looks!" she said.

"Dense," I replied, and Maddie chuckled.

We had arrived on a grassy hill, and below us sat some white cottages and a beautiful bay. A big sailboat was anchored in the middle of the bay, and a small one was tied to a wooden dock that jutted out from the shore. The skies were blue, and a few clouds meandered across, following the course set by a gentle breeze. It felt like one of those low-humidity spring days in the mountains.

I held Jack in my arms, and the dogs gathered closely around me. It was a peaceful place, but dogs take a while to adjust to new things.

"Wow, this is beautiful," I said.

"Thank you," said Maddie.

Just then, the Teacher disappeared, off to some other obligation, I guessed. He and I hadn't spoken, but I assumed he knew everything about me since he was one of them. It would take some time for me to get to know him, but eventually, I did, and I found him to be quite the enigma. He was an all-powerful alien but loved a human, who I believe you know already. Cynthia.

"Let's walk to town!" said Maddie. "By the way, this used to be called World 2B, but now we call it Neverland."

"Why Neverland?" I asked.

"Nothing grows old here," she said. "Even the children stay the same age they were when they arrived."

"What if a child wants to grow up?" I asked.

"Some do," she said. "And when that happens, we arrange for them to return to Earth. We find them a family that wants them, and then off they go."

"What if they want to return when they grow up?"

"I don't know," said Maddie. "It hasn't happened because we've only been operating the new and improved Earth Station for a few years."

"What about your children?" I asked. "Will they remain infants forever?"

"They would if they stayed here," said Maddie. "But eventually, we'll take them to live on Earth. Your assessment of how people feel about me there made me feel better about going."

I was happy to hear I'd helped Maddie but disturbed to learn she'd be going back to Earth. "What, you're going to leave me up here alone?" I asked.

"Not by yourself!" she said. "You have your dogs and Jack, and believe it or not, I think you'll meet people you want to be friends with up here."

"I don't do people very well," I said. "Except in my novels."

"You seem to get on well with me," she said, smiling, a twinkle in her eyes.

"Are you flirting with me, Maddie Pace?" I asked.

"Kind of," she said. "You're a handsome man, Zach. But the real point is that if you want a girlfriend, a boyfriend, or just plain old friends, there are plenty of good people here to choose from. You'll see."

It felt nice when she called me Zach. Few people ever took that leap with me because I'm such an oddball, living alone with nine dogs and a cat. But it would be nice if what Maddie said was true and I could meet some people that I liked. People who liked me back. And hopefully, they would call me Zach. So far, so good. And I had an in with the dogs by my side. I was a novelty as long as they were with me.

We passed by the four cottages on the way down the hill. Maddie told me the larger one would be where I would live. She explained that on World 2A, which was basically a twin of this island, the big house used to be called Human House because that's where the human bodies were made, but now it was just a residence over there and had always been a residence here on World 2B. She thought it would be a good house for me because it had a bedroom on the first floor and three on the upper floor, just like my home on Earth. She also pointed out that it was fully furnished. Even the dog beds were already in there. And a dog door had been installed with a smaller cat door embedded in the flap.

"I've left cat food and water out for Jack if you want to leave him there. He should be okay, right?"

"I think so," I said. "I'll tell him to wait around the area. It's okay if he goes outside, isn't it."

"Absolutely," she said.

I put Jack in the house, and we continued on, joining up with the road to town and leaving the bay behind. We passed by fields of crops and saw people working in them. The people looked up, saw us and the pack of dogs, and ran to the road to get a closer look. They were all so excited, which was a great feeling for me. I was already contributing to the quality of life here on Earth Station. Many people from the fields wanted to pet the dogs, which made my pack feel better. They'd been quite nervous and disoriented since we arrived, but the friendly welcome was helping. Nine tails wagged in unison as the farmers fawned over them. Hopefully, that would continue after the farmers experienced the phenomena of stepping in dog poop because that was inevitable. I couldn't clean up after nine of them and never had to, living in the woods. I told my dogs not to go whenever we were in town and to always go on the side of the road, not on the road itself. That was the best I could do.

As we came closer to town, I saw churches and temples lining the street. "You haven't suckered me into joining a cult, have you?" I asked Maddie.

She laughed. "Oh no. These buildings are left over from before, but some of them are being used. My mom attends church at that Protestant church right over there. Well, it's not Protestant anymore. It's a non-denominational church. She brought a pastor from Earth here to give the sermons and such. His name is Andy. Good guy. Not at all pushy about the religious stuff. People are free to practice their faiths if they want to. Or not. No one discriminates against others here just because of what they believe."

Maddie showed me the rest of town. The big brick building with columns up on a hill was an orphanage, but she cautioned that it wasn't to be called that. Its name was Neverland School and a big sign on the front announced that. Children of all shapes, sizes, and colors scampered around, playing. I wondered what it would be like to be a child forever. Just playing and enjoying life, not worrying about putting food on the table and taking care of others. Indeed, there were worse fates. But was life meant to be so…easy? I didn't know the answer to that one.

The town was lovely. Very clean. I wondered if the wine bar served beer, but I was hungry. "Can we eat in one of those restaurants?" I asked.

"We can," she said. "But Gino's preparing a big feast back home. We're neighbors, by the way. Gino and I live in one of the three smaller cottages near your house, my mom and the Teacher live in the other one, and my friend Gwen is staying in the third one right now. Can you wait until we get back there to eat?"

"That was a pretty long walk, wasn't it? I couldn't really tell."

"I have an idea," she said. "Do you think your dogs can find the way back to the enclave above the bay where we all live? If so, you and I can jump over, and the dogs can catch up soon."

"Absolutely," I said. "Tank is amazing with stuff like that. Wilson and Milo too. The rest of the pack will follow them, so they'll be fine once I tell them what to do. If we can get them some water first, then we can go."

Suddenly, three beautiful women that looked just like a younger Maddie (except they had hair) came out of the three restaurants, carrying bowls of water. They smiled and set them down in front of us. The dogs gathered around the three bowls and lapped up the water.

"Thank you," I said to the young women, wondering how that had happened.

"I sent them the message," said Maddie. "They're Imprints from the old Earth Station. They've been given the option to be reprogrammed to have a broader range of mental acuity, but they don't want to, so we're not going to force it on them."

"Interesting," I said.

"Shall we go?" asked Maddie, taking my hand.

I must admit that when she did that, I nearly fainted from the energy pulsing into me, probably influenced by my own attraction to her, but that was a street I didn't dare go down. And it didn't matter because we immediately popped out of existence and arrived back at the cottages.

Chapter 6

The neighborhood party was already in progress when we arrived. I hadn't noticed it before, but the three cottages were positioned in a way that they surrounded a communal backyard, in the center of which was an oversized patio paved with gray slate slabs of fieldstone. I could see my house just up the hill, which had a good view of the patio. It was a circle, maybe thirty feet in diameter, with a round wooden table in the center, surrounded by eight chairs. Two women were sitting at the table, along with the Teacher. Another man, presumably Gino, was over at the grill off to the side of the patio. A playpen sat between the grill and the table, and I guessed the twins were in there.

"Welcome!" yelled Gino, approaching me and extending his hand. "I'm Gino Morelli."

I shook his hand, gripping me like a boa constrictor squeezing its prey. "Zach Hurts," I said, deciding right then and there that I would be Zach from that point forward.

Gino released my hand. He was a few inches taller than me and had the body of Adonis. I stood no chance against Gino based on his looks and physique, but I didn't want to compete with him anyway. I was beginning to think that my attraction to Maddie was more like what my dogs and the animals in the forest felt. It was some kind of primal connection as if she were a biological magnet that attracted all other living things.

Gino kissed Maddie on the lips and waved me over toward the table. "Let's introduce you to everyone else," he said. We passed by the playpen, and Gino said, "In there are Casey and Tony, and I dare you to guess which one is which!" I peered in and smiled, and I would swear that both babies smiled back. They were in diapers with no shirts, just lying there watching the clouds go by. I noticed they were holding hands, which was adorable. "You know the Teacher, and this lady here is Maddie's mom, Cynthia."

Cynthia stood up and shook my hand, a big smile on her beautiful face. I was confused because, if anything, she looked younger than Maddie, and she was obviously a mind reader because she cleared that up right away. "Maddie marked me when I was twenty-seven," she said. "So that's how old I look. But I'm much older than that, although I'm not telling you my real age!"

"I'll be happy to tell you mine," said the other woman, standing and approaching me with her hand extended. "I'm Gwen, and I'm fifty-eight years old."

We shook hands, and I did a double take because the woman looked very familiar. "Hi, Gwen. Nice to meet you. I'm Zach."

Maddie cleared up my latest bout of confusion. "Yes, Gwen is the former President of the United States," she said. "But not up here!"

"And that's why I love Earth Station so much," said Gwen.

Gwendolyn Marks was tall and trim and had not a spec of gray in her dark hair, which she wore in a ponytail quite similar to mine. She was lying about being fifty-eight years old, or something else was up because she appeared to be in her mid-forties. An aura surrounded her that you could feel, and I suppose that's what people who rise to the top of their chosen fields have. Some kind of hutzpah that the rest of us are missing.

"I met your cat," she said.

"Oh, really? Do you know where he is? His name is Jack, by the way."

"One-eyed Jack!" she said. "He's a doll, Zach. He came and said hi and then went home."

Just then, the rest of the crew showed up. All nine of them, rolling in like a herd of buffalo, panting and slobbering all over the place. There was a little inflatable baby pool over in the grass, and they all veered in that direction, slurping from it with abandon.

"Sorry about that," I said. "I'll get that cleaned up right away."

I made a move toward the pool, but Gino stopped me. "No worries, dude. We'll clean that up later. We need to get you some kind of permanent watering trough for these guys. I'll build you one tomorrow."

"Thanks, Gino! I had one of those back on Earth, so you're definitely on the right track there."

"Hey, the burgers and dogs are just about ready," he said. "Why don't we all sit down and get ready to eat."

Maddie ran into a cottage and came out with a bowl of green salad and another of pasta salad. Gino brought the burgers and dogs over and put them beside the buns and condiments on the table.

"I thought you guys didn't eat red meat," I said. "Or did I hear that wrong, Maddie?"

"No, you got it right!" she said. "This is plant-based meat. I think you'll like it. By the way, what about the doggies? Do they need food?"

"To be honest, I'm having a little trouble keeping track of time up here," I said. "But based on my own growling stomach, I'd say that yes, they do."

At that instant, Maddie disappeared. A few minutes later, she reappeared. "Okay, their food is all set up in your house. And by the way, Jack is there. Perched on the sofa, looking out the window at us."

I picked up on Maddie's lead and told the dogs that dinner was waiting for them in our new home. They took off like a bolt of lightning, bunching up at the dog door to get in.

"Let's eat!" said Gino. "Tomorrow, we'll take you back to town so you can do some shopping."

"Do they sell plant-based bacon?" I asked, munching on a delicious burger.

"You bet!" said Gino.

The conversation was lively all evening, and the wine and beer flowed. Gino and I drank beer while everyone else had wine. The Teacher didn't talk much, but he seemed happy to be there, and so was I. I discovered that Gino and the Teacher had designed and built the large boat and that everyone in attendance, except myself, was an experienced sailor.

"I'll take you out sailing tomorrow if you'd like," said Gwen. "I can teach you the basics. On the small boat. The big one is a different animal, so we'll start small."

"Sounds great!" I said, and then I looked over at Maddie, who was beaming at me, trying to give me a sign by flicking her nonexistent eyebrows up and down. The thought crossed my mind that Maddie might have a little matchmaking on her mind, but there was no way the former President would go for a schmuck like me. On the other hand, I was definitely looking forward to tomorrow's sailing lesson.

Chapter 7

I woke up to a cacophony of knocking on my door. It was as if a crowd had gathered and were all knocking on the door simultaneously. I entered the main room and saw the dogs sitting there and looking nervous. I peeked out the window and determined that it actually was a crowd. A crowd of children. I opened the door and saw dozens of tiny faces staring at me.

"Can we play with your dogs, please?" asked a cute little boy with dark hair and brown skin.

I turned around to the dogs and asked them if they wanted to go out and play. If dogs could nod, they were nodding. Turning back to the kids, I said, "Okay, everybody, please step away from the door so the dogs can come out." The kids jumped back, I opened the door wide, and the stampede began. The next thing I knew, everyone was running and jumping and playing, and balls were being thrown, and it was an incredible sight.

I would never have been able to give this gift to my dogs back home. It was a good feeling. A validating feeling.

Soon after the kids arrived, Gino came over carrying a trough that looked too heavy for a human to move, but then I remembered that he was some kind of superhuman and probably didn't even feel it. The trough was six feet long by two feet wide by two feet deep, built from wood but sealed with something that made it watertight. "This ought to do it," he said, placing the trough in front of the house.

"Thank you, Gino!"

"There's a hose and a spigot right over here," he said. "We put that in just for you." He walked over to the spigot, turned it on, and dropped the hose into the trough.

Next to arrive was Gwen. She was wearing a swimsuit with a T-shirt over it, but oh my, were her legs long and firm. They must have done some age treatment on her because for a woman of fifty-eight, well, she looked darn good. Too good.

Gwen was carrying a picnic basket with her. "I brought some food for the sail," she said. "Even fried up some bacon for you and made a bacon and egg sandwich! The eggs are some kind of egg substitute, but they're delicious." Gwen kissed Gino on the cheek and looked up at me.

"Thank you, Gwen," I said, relived that I hadn't called her Madame President.

"Shall we go for a sail?" she asked.

"You bet!"

"See you later, Gino!" she said.

"Thanks again for the trough, dude!" I said, walking up to him and shaking his hand.

"My pleasure. You two have a nice sail!"

*****

Gino told me he'd keep an eye on the dogs, who were happily occupied at the moment. He explained that he would eventually ask the children to return to the Neverland School and promised to feed the dogs and Jack the cat. I thanked him, and Gwen and I walked down to the dock. She stepped onto the boat and placed the food basket on the floor. I wasn't a sailor then, so I didn't know the boat floor was called the sole.

"Untie the rope from the dock, okay?" she asked.

I untied the rope, threw it on board, and then joined Gwen on the boat. She pulled a rope that raised the sail and tied it down on what I learned was called a cleat, then made her way to the back of the boat. There was another roped tied down there that allowed her to decide how much the boom could move to the side. She untied it and held it in her hand, giving the boom a slight push to the left side of the boat. The sail caught the wind, and she tied the rope down and steered us out of the bay.

"Have you ever sailed before?" she asked.

"No, I haven't, but it seems simple enough," I said. "There's the two ropes and the steering mechanism, which seems to be it."

"Sort of," she said. "For this boat. But there are a lot of nautical terms you should know. The front of the boat is called the bow; the back is the stern. The right side is the starboard, and the left is the port. The steering mechanism is called a tiller. The maneuver we just executed is called a starboard tack because the wind is blowing into the sail from the starboard side of the boat. When the wind direction changes relative to the boat, we might have to perform a port tack and allow the sail to catch the wind from the port side."

"Got it," I said. "Easy, peasy."

She smiled. "I forgot that you're an Imprint. Photographic memory." Being called an Imprint shook me slightly, and I must have frowned because Gwen noticed. "I'm sorry," she said. "Maddie told me the whole story about you not knowing where you're from and all of that. I'm sure it's still fresh in your mind."

Gwen's sensitivity made me feel better, and frankly, I'd gotten used to the fact that I was technically an Imprint, but the reality was that I felt utterly human, and I said as much. "Yes, it seems I was made here, but my entire life was spent on Earth, so I'm really no different than you. And I've lost most of my abilities, except the memory, and I can talk with animals."

"I love your dogs and Jack," she said. "I had pets growing up, but in my adult life, they've been absent. I didn't realize how much I missed that until you and your pack showed up."

"I'm the opposite," I said. "No pets growing up and nothing but pets as an adult."

We stopped talking for a while, and Gwen steered the boat to the port after we left the bay. I noticed fins in the water, and an alarm went off in my head. "Are those sharks?" I asked.

"Yeah," she said. "Can you talk to them?"

I tried and failed to communicate with the sharks. "Seems not," I said.

"Well, if you could, you would find they're friendly. I'm told that at one time, they were programmed to kill humans because this island used to be inhabited by some very aggressive and ambitious people who would often try to leave the island. The sharks were a deterrent, and I'm told very few people died because people aren't stupid, right?"

I don't know why, but I struggled to believe the sharks were friendly. Gwen seemed to pick up on that. "Come here and steer the boat for a minute, okay, Zach?"

She stood up, and I moved to take the tiller from her. Then she pulled off her T-shirt. I felt my eyebrows rise up. She was wearing a one-piece swimsuit, but it couldn't hide that she was a shapely woman. Oh man, it had been too long for me. I was a basket case just looking at her. Suddenly, she went to the front of the boat and dove into the water. A few sharks approached her, and I was terrified for her, but then the sharks just nudged up beside her, and she started petting two of them. Then she turned horizontally and began swimming rapidly in the same direction as the boat, which was moving past her now. She grabbed onto the side and hauled herself up, putting her hands to her face and pushing her wet hair back. The water glistened on her body, and I was further shaken by the sight of her.

"Okay, now are you convinced that the sharks are friendly?" she asked, sitting on the bench at the front of the boat. I nodded my head. "If you get to know me, Zach, you'll learn that I'm an open book. I have difficulty lying."

"Oh, that's different," I said. "Especially for a politician. But it obviously worked for you. You made it all the way to the top. Do you miss it?"

She didn't hesitate. "Very much."

"What do you miss about it, Gwen? I mean, it's a pretty high-pressure job. Are you saying you liked that?"

"I did. I love it when my adrenaline gets going and I'm facing an impossible situation. My mind reaches a clarity during those times that is far and away the biggest rush I've ever had. It's like a drug addiction, at least for me. I always wanted more, and I've been looking for more ever since I left office. That's why I came to Earth Station. I thought I'd find it here."

"And did you?"

"The World of the Makers is pretty cool," she said. "But they don't like people hanging around over there, so the only Maker I know well is the Teacher. Neverland is wonderful, but it can get kind of boring after a while. At least for me, that's what happened. Cynthia loves it here, but Maddie and Gino seem to feel more like I do."

"How long do you plan on staying here?" I asked.

"Well, first of all, I haven't been approved as a permanent resident of Earth Station. They give priority to the underprivileged and to Imprints. But I could be approved if I wanted to be."

"What would you do if you left?" I asked.

She shook her head. "I don't know," she said. "I just want more."

"More action? More excitement?"

"For sure," she said.

I was at a loss in terms of making any suggestions to Gwen about how to get more excitement in her life. As for myself, just being in her presence rivaled anything I'd ever experienced, including meeting Maddie. "I hope you stay for a while," I said, and I felt blood rushing to my cheeks.

"Oh, I will," she said. "After all, I hardly know your pack, and they're the most exciting thing that's happened here since I've been around."

I was happy to hear that and wondered if she considered me a pack member too.

Chapter 8

The Teacher came to see me shortly after Gwen and I returned to Neverland. He asked me if they could study my brain to see what the lightning had done to change my programming. I asked him if that was why they had brought me to Earth Station, and he gave me an interesting response.

"Maddie wanted you here, and what Maddie wants, she gets. If there is a God of Earth Station, she is it."

I wanted to explore that idea further with the Teacher, but he steered the conversation back to his original purpose. He told me the scan of my brain would take only a few minutes. I explained that I would be happy to do it but was wondering if, in exchange, he would help old Jenny to feel less pain in her joints. The other dogs all seemed fine, so I didn't ask for anything for them. He readily agreed and then whisked me away to some massive complex in a valley between two mountain ranges.

He explained that Mountain Lake was on the other side of one range and recommended that I visit there with the dogs, telling me it would remind me of the mountain lake at my home in New Hampshire. He also said there would be a surprise waiting for me there when I arrived.

As promised, the scan took less than five minutes. The Teacher would use it to replicate my ability to communicate with animals and enhance it to include a greater range of species. He promised to keep me informed. When I returned to my house, I let the dogs out and went to Gwen's cottage. I asked her if she'd like to go to Mountain Lake with us, and she said yes, telling me we could pick up a swimsuit for me in town, which was on the way to the lake.

The lake was beautiful, as promised, perhaps more beautiful than my lake in the White Mountains. It was nestled right into the mountains, whereas the mountains were further away from my lake in New Hampshire. When we got to the beach, Gwen introduced me to the people there, and everyone gathered around the dogs. The lab mixes and the retriever took to the water immediately, and the non-water lovers in the pack, led by Wilson, drank from it but didn't go swimming. My first surprise was a school of ducks swimming nearby. I remembered Maddie had gotten a scan of a duck on my lake and was amazed that it had been recreated into several of them. Next, I saw a family of otters playing in the distance, and further out was a beaver lodge.

"I'm told there are bears, coyotes, and bobcats nearby, too," said Gwen. "Say, you want to go for a swim?" She stripped out of her T-shirt and shorts, revealing a bikini.

I couldn't help myself. "Gwen, may I ask you a personal question?"

"You can ask, but I can't promise I'll answer." She was grinning, already wading into the water.

"Okay. I'm wondering how you've managed to look so good as you've grown older. Fifty-eight isn't old, but it's older than you seem to be."

Gwen smiled. "I was always a workout fiend," she said. "And I eat well."

"Anything else?"

"Maddie marked me when I was forty-eight years old, the first time we met, in the Oval Office. Not long after I came here, I asked if they could make a new me based on that marking, and they said they could. They asked me not to broadcast it because they were worried that the older people here might be lining up to see if they'd been marked by an unknown Imprint somewhere along the way." She raised her index finger to her lips, signaling me to keep it quiet, and I nodded in compliance.

"Can you read minds too?"

"No, but I'm really strong. Not as strong as Maddie because she's had some special treatments that no one else has had, but I'm as strong as Gino and Cynthia. I didn't want the mind reading function turned on because I think it takes away too much of the mystery of meeting new people."

"That's good to know. I actually thought you could read minds because you seem to know what I'm thinking before I say it."

She thought about this. "You're not exactly my type, Zach, but we have a connection. Just like Maddie said there would be."

I didn't know whether to be depressed because I wasn't Gwen's type or elated because she said we had a connection. "Did Maddie bring me here just to meet you?" I asked.

"I don't think so. But she's been worried about me, for sure. I've been worried about me too."

"What's wrong?"

"Just what I said before. I'm looking for that energy I found when I was President. Not so easy to find, though."

"I'll give it some thought," I said. "You know I'm a pretty imaginative sort, with my writing and all."

"Great!" she said, and she seemed to mean it. "Anyway, it's nice to get to know each other a little bit at a time. You know what I mean?"

I felt my eyebrows go up but wasn't afraid to answer because the truth was easy to tell. "Absolutely," I said.

Upon our return to town, Gwen and I stopped at the Wine Bar for a drink. She ordered white wine, and I ordered a beer, which they had, thank goodness. I'm not so big on wine. We toasted, and Gwen had something new to tell me.

"Gino and Maddie are planning a trip on the big boat. You and I are invited. If you want to go, Cynthia and the Teacher will look after the dogs. In fact, Cynthia was wondering if you'd allow her to bring the dogs to the school where she works. Would that be okay?"

"Definitely. And I'd love to go on a trip on the big boat. Do they have a specific plan of where they want to go?"

"I don't know all the details," she said. "But I know that Gino wants to do something he's never done before."

"What?"

"He wants to sail around the world."

Chapter 9

W e brought enough food and water to last for several months, although Gino pointed out that there would be places along our course where we could replenish our supplies if needed. The circumference of Earth Station was around seven thousand miles, just slightly greater than the moon's circumference. Based on an average wind speed of six knots (which wasn't much, but was a fact of life on Earth Station; gentle breezes were the norm all over the planet), Gino estimated it would take around fifty days to make it all the way around if we didn't stop along the way. But he intended to make port a few times so we could experience some of the new places constructed on Earth Station since the change of direction in its purpose. It used to be a place where human Essences were collected, studied, perfected, and ultimately, blended with Maker Essences or discarded. But that time was over now.

The planet had become a refuge for real humans, most of them having been disenfranchised on Earth, and for Imprints like myself whose purpose on Earth had been abandoned.

The boat was named "Bella," after Gino's mom, who had passed away some time ago. I also learned that Tony, Maddie and Gino's son, had been named after his father, Antonio, who had also moved on. I was led to believe that Gino struggled daily with his yearning to see his family again and suffered mightily when word came to him of each of his parent's passing. He still had two brothers and a sister on Earth, but they were getting older. Gino himself would be sixty-four Earth years old if he hadn't been reborn as a thirty-one-year-old.

But back to the boat, which according to Gino, was a dream vessel. Literally, born out of his dreams and constructed with the help of the Teacher, who had access to a vast factory (the lab where they had done my testing was in the same gigantic building) that could build virtually anything. The boat was fifty feet long and was powered by two sails, a mainsail, and a genoa. The front deck of the vessel was huge, and if there had been a sun on Earth Station, it would have been an excellent place for sunbathing. Nevertheless, we often gathered there and played cards and other games. Maddie was impossible to beat because she cheated! Reading minds is cheating in my book.

The cockpit of the boat was aft, and it was open and had seating to accommodate all four of us at once. Gino loved to sail, but he gave all of us a chance, and with the autopilot function, we could maneuver the boat without all the work that used to be part of sailing a big boat like that. We just pushed buttons to execute all the movements of the sails, although from time to time, Gino would turn off the autopilot and make us work the winches and ropes, sailing like the old days.

Down below was marvelous. There were four large cabins, each with its own shower and toilet. Maddie and Gino shared one, Gwen and I each had our own cabin, and one was empty, but we stored a lot of foodstuffs and 5-gallon bottles of fresh water in there because the galley, while large and spacious, couldn't hold three months' worth of supplies. The saloon, the communal area below deck where we could all gather, was spacious and comfortable, with two built-in sofas and a few chairs bolted down to the floor. However, we didn't use it much because there was no night on Earth Station, and the seas were never rough. Plus, it never rained, and the temperature was always seventy-two degrees Fahrenheit. In other words, there was no reason to be inside.

Along the way south, we passed by several new islands still being settled, wanting to avoid disturbing the process or confusing people about who we might be. One day, Gino pulled down the sails and motored into the harbor of a new island that he said was an extraordinary place.

"It's called Atlantis," he said.

"Why?" I asked.

"It's supposed to be a utopia, but a special kind. The only people who live there are either highly creative or highly analytical. You can see that it's basically two islands with a wide channel between them. The creative people live on one side and the analytical people on the other."

It was obvious which side the Creatives lived on and which the Analyticals lived on. The island on the left was full of buildings with dramatic curves and unique surfaces, while the island on the right was filled with symmetrically aligned buildings with straight sides and 90-degree turns from side to side.

"Do they ever get together?" I asked, wondering how this could be a utopia being divided up in this way.

"Yes," he said. "Do you see the island up ahead in the center of the channel? And the bridges from each of the two main islands that connect everything? That's where they come together. It's the place where the people of both islands work."

"What do they work on?"

"They're trying to create things that humans have never created before without the Makers' help. They're working on space travel, food production, holographic art, you name it, they probably have a project on it."

Then Maddie chimed in. "If you get bored in Neverland, Zach, you can apply to live here. I've read all your books, and you have the talent to be here."

I smiled and nodded but had no desire to live in such a place. My mind was on more basic things at the moment. Most of my waking thoughts surrounded Gwen, although Maddie wasn't helping either. Both wore bikinis 24/7, which was very disconcerting for someone who hadn't been around women for many years. On the positive side, it proved that I still was attracted to women and definitely felt able to perform if the opportunity presented itself. But it seemed that wasn't going to happen any time soon. I spent hours thinking about what Gwen meant when she'd said, "It's nice to get to know each other a little bit at a time." How much time was she thinking, I wondered? And was the "connection" she felt we had the same one I thought we had? So far, it seemed the answer was no.

We made port on the center island in Atlantis and were given a tour of the cities. The humans living here all knew who Maddie was because they had all been on Earth when Maddie had been introduced to the world by Gwen back in 2029, and their deference to her suggested nothing but adoration. More evidence to suggest the Teacher's words about Maddie being a "God" here on Earth Station were not simply idle speculation. At any rate, the Creatives and the Analyticals seemed to mesh together well; other than the more elaborate garb of the Creatives, it was hard to tell which was which. I looked forward to seeing what fabulous inventions they would come up with here on Atlantis and had no doubt there would be many.

The next place we passed by was the World of the Makers. It had the shape of a volcanic island, but I was told the top was solid and the place where the Council of the Makers met to make decisions on important matters.

"I'd like to see that," I said.

Just then, Maddie stepped up to me and took my hand, and off we went. We popped into existence on top of the great mountain we had just seen from the boat, and I had a 360-degree view of the water surrounding the island.

"The boat is out there," she said, pointing at it. I thought I saw it, but my vision wasn't as acute as hers. I'd been told that my original programming gave me 20/5 vision, but the lightning did away with that as well. "Over on this side, down below, is the Empath Village," she said, walking to one side of the great circle. I followed her and looked over the edge. The Empath Village looked like the enclave where the four of us, plus the Teacher and Cynthia, lived, only larger. "Now, come over here to the other side." She dragged me over there, and I looked down on a neighborhood that looked more like Malibu, California, than anything else. Massive dwellings dotted the hillside. "The Village of the Selfs," she said.

"Wow, big difference," I said.

"One of many," she said, frowning. "I don't like the Selfs. They shouldn't be here, in my opinion."

"Where should they be, Maddie?"

"Nowhere."

She took my hand, and then we were back on the boat.

"Thank you," I said.

"My pleasure," she said, smiling.

"Where to next?" I asked.

"The South Pole," said Gino.

Chapter 10

It was a long sail from the World of the Makers to the South Pole, but I have no idea how long. Time was a mystery to me on Earth Station, as it was to everyone else. It seemed as if time was passing, but since there was only day and no night, it was impossible to gauge. I didn't own a watch myself, but I would have thought someone here would have one, but no one did, and I wondered if a watch would even work here since time didn't move. Probably so, and I imagine the Makers could invent a watch or a clock that would work here even if a regular watch didn't. On the other hand, why should they? To them, time didn't matter. Perhaps the inventors of Atlantis would come up with something. When I first arrived, I wanted to know how much time was passing, but the longer I was here, the less it mattered to me.

Gino explained that there were no land masses on Earth Station south of the World of the Makers. He also commented that "south" was a convenience he'd adopted to help navigate and that he had no idea if there really was a southerly direction since he didn't know anything about the positioning of the station in space. And it didn't matter. South was the direction we were heading, and that's all we needed to know.

Gino mentioned something that I found somewhat confusing and disconcerting. He said we wouldn't be able to transit directly over the South Pole because the waters surrounding it were off-limits to any form of transit—by sea, air, or teleportation.

"What goes on there that makes it off-limits?" I asked.

"Apparently, it's the area where large shipments from other parts of the Megaverse are brought in. Raw materials for building things and stuff like that."

"Hmmm," I said, wondering if that was all that went on there.

One day (and I say "one day" simply out of habit because it was one endless day here, all the time), Gwen and I were lounging on the forward deck while Maddie and Gino manned the cockpit aft. She was sipping wine, and I was drinking a can of beer. Gwen casually reached over and took my free hand in hers. She was grinning, and her eyes twinkled with mischief. Then she leaned over and whispered in my ear. "Want to go below and fool around?"

I was at a loss for words. The best I could do was nod my head. Then I stood up, undoubtedly faster than I should, and went straight for the stairs. When I got below, I realized I hadn't asked her which cabin she wanted to use, so I waited in the hallway, somewhat embarrassed that I wasn't handling this with a little more aplomb. She came down, a broad smile on her pretty face, and walked into her cabin. I followed like a puppy after its mother, and as I entered her room, I watched her strip off her bikini top and bottom. I followed her lead and got out of my swimsuit, and we sat beside each other on the bed.

Gwen looked me in the eye. "Been a while, huh?"

"Longer than I can remember," I said.

"Me too," she whispered, and that made me feel better.

We moved toward each other, and our lips met, slowly pressing against each other. She opened her mouth, and I followed. We embraced, and I felt the intimate presence of another human being merging with my own. She inhaled a sharp breath of desire through her nose, then lay back on the bed. After that, I don't remember much, but I feel like we were together in that bed for a long time. When we finally finished, Gwen was open with me, as always.

"I thought you said you weren't strong like I am," she said. "Because there were times when you seemed extremely strong to me!"

I remembered one moment when she was on top of me, and I lifted her entire body into the air and laid her down beside me, then rolled on top of her. I remembered her legs feeling like iron as she clasped me within them, but my own legs held their own, the balance between us seeming perfect. Who knows, maybe I did have the strength that all the manufactured beings here had. But it didn't matter. Gwen and I had made love, and it was beautiful. I'd been alone for so long, and could never have dreamed of such an ideal partner to end my long abnegation.

*****

The world changed when Gwen and I went up on deck and joined Maddie and Gino in the cockpit. I saw a massive power boat approaching us at high speed, and it looked like four people were on board. They all looked like replicas of the Teacher.

"It's Gabriel and some of his Self brethren," said Maddie, frowning as if she knew it was trouble.

"Who's Gabriel?" I asked.

"He's a Self Maker. Probably the most obnoxious one since Sidorov. I can't stand the guy."

The power boat arched in a half circle and throttled down to come alongside us. I heard the powerful engine grinding down, and now they were pulling along beside us at six knots, our perpetual speed. One of them spoke, and I assumed it was Gabriel.

"You realize you're approaching an off-limits zone, don't you?" he yelled.

Gino, our captain, answered. "We're nowhere near that zone, Gabriel, and you know it."

"You're closer than you think. Close enough to come to our attention. I am ordering you to turn your boat around and head back to where you came from."

"On whose authority?" asked Gino.

"The Council of the Makers. We are the authorized patrol boat for this area. You are ordered to turn around now."

"Furl the sails," Maddie whispered. "Then drop the anchor."

Gino executed the instructions.

Gabriel saw what was happening. "Do you think two remade humans, a malfunctioning Imprint and a Maker wannabe are a match for four Makers?"

"You mean Half Breed Makers, don't you?" yelled Maddie, taking over the conversation for our side. At the same moment, Maddie's voice came into my head. *Come close to me*, she said. When everyone stepped near her, I realized she'd sent the same thought to all of us. I felt a throbbing pass through me, and then it was gone. Some kind of energy burst.

"Do you really think your pathetic shield can stop us?" asked Gabriel.

"I'm just giving you the opportunity to take the first punch, Gabe," said Maddie, relaxed and smiling.

All eight of us knew that Maddie had killed the most powerful Self of all time. Sidorov. But that had been a one-on-one battle. There were four of these Selfs. It was a game of chicken, but Maddie was known as a great gambler. I waited for the blast from the other boat, but it didn't come. Instead, Gabriel turned away, got behind the wheel, threw the throttle up, roaring away from us, the wake of the power boat tipping our sailboat precariously. But the reliable vessel righted itself quickly, and then we were alone.

Gwen broke the silence. "Can you track him?" she asked Gino.

"Sure," he said. "But why?"

"Let's see where they go. I have a hunch they're not returning to World of the Makers. Not now, at least."

Gino turned on the radar, and we gathered around, watching the screen. He made some adjustments, and the circular off-limits area surrounding the South Pole appeared in the center of the screen. Off to the right of the circle was Gabriel's boat, moving in a westerly direction. Our boat was shown as a stationary object. There were no other vessels on the screen. We were on our own down here at the bottom of the world.

After a few minutes, it became clear that Gabriel's boat was tracing a line around the off-limits zone, close to it but never crossing over. When his boat was 180 degrees around the circle, at the farthest point from us it could be, Gabriel's boat approached the boundary of the off-limits circle, then crossed over it and disappeared from the screen.

"The radar doesn't work inside the off-limits zone," said Gino.

"But they went in there!" said Gwen, excited. "They're breaking the law. We need to stop them."

I wasn't sure where Gwen's excitement was coming from, but something told me it might have something to do with her need for a new challenge. She'd just witnessed her best friend beat four Makers in a game of chicken, so this must have buoyed her confidence, but it didn't make sense to me to take such as risk.

"We can't catch them," said Gino. "Why even try? Plus, we don't know what's inside that zone. It might be harmful to us. Maybe even deadly."

But Gwen persisted. "They went in there. Why would they do that if the place is harmful? Look, guys, something is going on in there, and my gut tells me we need to find out what. My gut is never wrong. We'll be fine. Maddie, what do you think?"

All of us knew that Maddie would make the call on whether to breach the off-limits barrier or not. Gino was the captain, but Maddie was the unquestioned leader of this group. Perhaps the leader of all of Earth Station. I once again reflected on the Teacher's comment about Maddie. "If there is a God of Earth Station, she is it."

What this meant was that we weren't voting on this. If Maddie said to go, then we were going. Period.

"Let's do it," she said.

Without a word, Gino pushed the button to pull up the anchor, then the ones to hoist the sails. He set the heading directly for the South Pole. We would soon cross over the off-limits boundary and learn our fate.

Chapter 11

The radar began to function again when we passed into the off-limits zone. Sort of. The image on the screen was fuzzy, and the circle we were in couldn't hold its shape. It pulsed in and out, and the boundary became wavy, fluctuating wildly. But the point on the map that was Gabriel's vessel was there, heading directly for the South Pole. Gino was making a direct heading for the pole as well. Since Gabriel's boat had entered on the other side of the circle, we were heading directly at each other now, but they would reach the pole far sooner than us. The distance we had to travel was approximately fifty nautical miles, which would take around eight hours to transit at our speed. Our adversaries would reach the pole in only one hour as they powered forward at fifty knots compared to our paltry six.

One hour later, we were all glued to the radar screen, watching to see what Gabriel's boat did when they reached the pole. But we didn't expect what happened. The instant they crossed directly over the pole, their boat disappeared from the radar screen.

"What just happened?" asked Gwen.

"Not sure," said Gino. "It doesn't seem to be a radar malfunction. What do you guys think we should do now?"

"Keep the heading," said Maddie, and the matter was resolved.

Seven hours later, we crossed over the pole. There was nothing but water as far as the eye could see. There was no loading and unloading zone, so I wondered how these "supplies" were transported here and then moved to their final destination on Earth Station. More importantly, I felt a slight, nearly imperceptible tremor when we crossed over the pole.

"Did anyone feel that?" I asked.

Everyone nodded, but our boat just kept sailing ahead. There was no sign of Gabriel's boat. Just endless water.

"Anyone have any suggestions about what to do next?" asked Gino.

Everyone's eyes turned to Maddie. "Let's go home," she said. "Sail us out of this zone and then circle back the way we came. Things have gotten too strange. We need to speak with the Teacher about this."

That made sense to me, and Gino apparently agreed because he followed Maddie's instructions without saying anything. There was nothing to do then, so we sailed on, left the off-limits zone, and the radar started acting right again. None of us understood what we had seen when Gabriel's boat disappeared from the radar. Had it sunk? Had there been a malfunction? We simply didn't know.

Needless to say, it was a long trip back, and the excitement of the first part of our journey had been replaced by anxiety. All of us knew something was wrong. At the very least, Earth Station wasn't what we had thought it was; at least the South Pole wasn't. We needed answers, and only the Teacher could give them to us.

After some interminable time, we passed by the World of the Makers. We were a good distance away, so even the powerful eyesight of certain crew members couldn't make out any details.

"Do you think we should check to see if Gabriel's boat has returned?" asked Gino.

"Not all the beings there are our friends," said Maddie. "We need to speak to the Maker who is."

Maddie was right, as always, but we didn't know then that the Teacher wouldn't be waiting for us if and when we reached Neverland. We got our first clue something was amiss when we passed the area where Atlantis was supposed to be.

"Guys," said Gino. "Atlantis isn't there."

"What are you talking about?" asked Gwen.

Gino pulled up a screen that showed all the islands in this part of the world. He noted the coordinates of Atlantis, then showed us those coordinates on the radar screen. There was nothing there. All of us had quick minds, and each of us knew intuitively what needed to happen next.

"I'm going to Neverland now," said Maddie. "I'll be back soon and tell you what I find."

Some amount of time went by. How much? Who knows? I certainly didn't. The three of us waited, nervous, knowing something was very wrong with our situation. Suddenly, Maddie reappeared.

"This isn't Earth Station!" she said. "At least it's not our Earth Station."

"How do you know?" I asked.

"The Teacher wasn't there. Neither was Cynthia. And your dogs weren't either."

"Maybe they're at the school," I said.

"There is no friggin' school! And the people, they're all different."

"How so?" I asked.

"They're all five feet tall, for one thing. And they look more primitive, somehow. I knew we needed more information, so I went to the Monitoring Station. It's still there. I blasted in there and saw maps on the wall, just like ours, except the people working there were all five feet tall. I read a few of their minds and learned that we're in a star system twelve light years from Earth!"

"What the fuck?" said Gwen. "You mean the South Pole is some kind of transporting station. Well, if that's true, then Gabriel must be here. Let's go back to the World of the Makers. At this point, Gabriel might be our best friend."

"I've already been to the World of the Makers," said Maddie. "And guess what? They're all five feet tall too! There was no sign of Gabriel. And I have to tell you guys. The Makers weren't happy to see me at all."

"What did they do?" asked Gino.

"They tried to stun me!" she said. "But I was able to get my shield up, and then I flashed out of there. But I don't think we can avoid them for long. They know something isn't right, just like we do."

Right on cue, the sound of a fleet of powerful boats reached our ears. In the distance, we saw a dozen power boats speeding toward us. When the boats got closer, they ran in a circle, surrounding us. All of the occupants were wearing the long robes of the Makers, but they were short and had exaggerated brows. They looked like cavemen, if I'm honest.

"Come close to me," said Maddie.

We all complied, and her shield went up just in time. We felt blasts coming at us from all sides, and I wondered how long Maddie's energy would hold up. My guess was not much longer.

Maddie screamed something, and I also heard it in my head simultaneously. "We are from Earth Station in the Sol system! Bring the Master of Earth Station here. He will vouch for us."

The blasts stopped. And we waited.

Chapter 12

The Teacher appeared on our boat sometime later. He was shaking his head in frustration, a rarity for him, so I am told.

"Maddie, my dearest child, it seems you have wandered off the reservation."

"Well said, Teacher," she replied. "But you've got a lot of explaining to do."

"Fine," he said. "Give me a few moments with my colleagues, will you, and then I will take us home."

Going home to Earth Station was all I needed to hear. This interstellar travel wasn't for me. The Teacher had some kind of a thought conversation with the five-foot-tall Makers and then turned back to us.

"Everyone hold hands, please," he said.

"But what about the boat?" asked Gino as we all clasped hands.

"The boat will be fine," said the Teacher.

"But I love this…"

A microsecond later, we arrived back at the South Pole of the Station we had been transported to from Earth Station. How did I know this? I didn't then, but the Teacher later explained it to us. From there, the portal took us back to the South Pole of Earth Station, and from there, the Teacher moved us to the bay at Neverland. On the shore, I saw my nine dogs barking at us and Cynthia waving. We were standing on the deck of the boat, which had obviously come with us. The power of the Teacher seemed to have no bounds. I thought he could only move people, but he'd just demonstrated he could also carry a fifty-foot sailboat. The portal between stations had done most of the work, but The Teacher had crossed a distance on the surface of the stations in an instant, with us and the boat in tow, that had taken us weeks to sail. I marveled at his power to harness the energy to accomplish such things.

The Teacher took Gino to shore; Maddie took Gwen, and I. Cynthia hugged Maddie first and then the rest of us. "I've got a meal waiting," she said. "And plenty of wine and beer. We can eat on the patio."

My dogs were happy to see me, but not overly so. They seemed utterly content with Cynthia, which made me a little jealous.

As we gathered around the table on the patio, the cold beer tasted as good as I can remember a beer ever tasting to me. I felt like I'd been on the adventure of a lifetime, survived, and was now home. Yes, Earth Station was my home, not the White Mountains. I wanted to stay there but also wanted to be with Gwen, which was my undoing. It began with a story the Teacher told us, in thought-speak, about what humans really were:

Please save your questions for later. Most will be answered if you listen to what I say. First, let me speak of the beings you saw at Gilese Station. That star system is twelve light years from the Sol system. Those humans are at a much less advanced stage than humans on Earth. The comparable term for them in Earth terminology is Homo Erectus. The final stage of evolution before Homo Sapiens.

There are humans, in various stages of development, throughout the Milky Way galaxy, and also in the nearby Canis Major Dwarf galaxy, and in the Draco II galaxy. How many planets have human life on them, you ask? Tens of thousands. Humans are the most prevalent species in the Milky Way galaxy by far and are close to attaining that status in Canis and Draco. How could that happen?

The Makers know where human life began, which wasn't on Earth. It began on a planet 580 light years from Earth, known in Earth astronomy as Kepler 186f. Kepler 186 is a red dwarf star, and the planet 186f is the fifth planet from its sun. It is 11% larger than Earth and contains liquid water that covers 90% of its surface. While it is much closer to its sun than Earth is to Sol, Kepler 186 is not as luminous as Sol and therefore produces temperatures perfect for the development of life on this planet. The closest English translation to what these humans call their planet is Aria. They are musical people and often communicate by singing, although they can speak and hear telepathically using AI for assistance. Intelligent life developed on Aria millions of years before it did on Earth, and it is no coincidence that one of the intelligent life forms on their planet, beings that could speak, socialize and worship a deity, looked very much like Homo Erectus on Earth. Of course, they took the next step to Homo Sapiens, as does every planet where Homo Erectus appears, which is literally everywhere human life has evolved.

How do these primitive humans get to all of these planets? Of course, they are placed there by the Arian race, who discovered light-speed travel over fifty thousand years ago and have discovered how to recreate their ancient ancestors. Thus, they have been seeding the Milky Way and nearby galaxies with the essential precursor of human life for all that time. Why, you ask, do they do this? Because they want to survive, my friends. The universe is not a friendly place, so by seeding the galaxies with human life, the Arians believed they were protecting themselves; at least, they thought they were. The logic was that members of their own species would never want to harm their own. Of course, that logic is flawed.

Look at Earth. If not for the Makers, humans on Earth may have already destroyed themselves. Humans can be very aggressive, you see, against their own kind or against other species. This tendency toward physically aggressive behavior never happened on Aria; at least, they say it didn't, so in theory, they had no reason to expect it to happen elsewhere. But, of course, it did, and it does. Why? We are studying that. It seems the reason is due to environmental factors common on any given planet. Harsh weather conditions, other species that are aggressive hunters, etc. We have not been able to study these factors on Aria itself for reasons I will explain later. Regardless, If there ever was a natural utopia in the universe, Aria is it, from what we are told and from the observations we can make from space.

I should explain what I was thinking while the Teacher was describing this world, Aria, where humans supposedly originated. First, the word's pronunciation is *Ahr-ee-uh*, as I'm sure most of you know. And it follows that the pronunciation of the word for the beings who live there, Arians, is *Ahr-ee-uns*. But a similar word popped into my mind as the Teacher was going through his explanation: Aryan, as in the Aryan Race, pronounced *Air-ee-un*. This, of course, was the race that Hitler espoused as being the Master Race of mankind on Earth back in the twentieth century. I remember wondering at the time the Teacher was telling us about this alleged utopia if the similarity between the two words, Arian and Aryan, was a coincidence or if there was more to it. I'll tell more about what we discovered later, but I thought it might be helpful to convey now my fleeting thoughts when first exposed to the word Arian (remember, it's pronounced *Ahr-ee-un*). But now I return to the Teacher's closing remarks on that day:

So, we continue to study humanity on tens of thousands of worlds, fascinated by this species, which demonstrates a propensity for variation which has never been seen in the Megaverse before. It's also interesting that our Humanity Project is a joint venture with the Arians. All the stations, such as this one, are built by them in the space surrounding the uninhabited planets of their solar system and then transported to their final destination by the Pathways throughout the Megaverse. We have granted access to the Pathways to the Arians, affording them the ability to travel rapidly to wherever they want to go rather than submit themselves to stasis for hundreds, even thousands, of years at a time.

Now, questions.

Maddie was first. "Why didn't you tell us?"

"That question, my dear Maddie, is best answered by the thought bursting from your friend Gwen's mind."

Gwen didn't give Maddie the chance to read her mind. "I want to go there," she said. "I want to go to Aria."

Chapter 13

So much for my hopes and dreams. I had only moments ago wondered how I could talk Gwen into making a life here on Earth Station with me, and now she'd decided that she wanted to go to a planet 580 light years away. But before I tell you how that matter concluded, let me clean up a few loose ends you may have been wondering about.

The South Pole of Earth Station, and every other similar station built to study humans, was a gateway to the other stations. If anyone crossed over the pole without initiating the proper programming sequence, they would be moved to the next closest station. In our case, that station was only twelve light years away, which in galactic terms is quite close.

Unbeknownst to us was the ongoing program the Makers employed to give the Empath Makers and Self Makers experience in the universe beyond Earth Station, theoretically as preparation for becoming a Maker with full privileges to travel the Megaverse. Any Empath or Self Maker could apply for transit to a specific planet among the tens of thousands in the "Humanity Project" and go there to interact with the local Makers, learning about the customs of the world in question and their differences from Earth humans. Once approved, they were given a programming sequence to make the visit. This is what Gabriel had been doing when he confronted us. His mistake was being so anxious to go that he risked being followed by our group, which is what happened.

Needless to say, we were all sworn to secrecy by the Teacher, under threat of having the memories of the entire incident removed. None of us had any reason to tell anyone, especially Gwen, who wanted more than anything to be approved for transit to Aria, the birthplace of humanity. You might be surprised to hear that the Teacher didn't fight this request with much enthusiasm. There was no arm-twisting from Cynthia and Maddie needed. In fact, he said there were reasons the Makers would welcome a trip like this from someone other than themselves and promised to discuss this later.

The trip was approved, but Gwen would need some reprogramming to make the most of her visit. Teacher's orders. He elaborated that the Makers had open contact with the people of Aria, as this was one of the most advanced civilizations in the Megaverse. He suggested that Gwen's visit could be portrayed as a quasi-diplomatic mission due to her status as a former President of the most powerful nation on Earth. On the other hand, he cautioned that it was best not to involve Earth, giving assurances that he could set the whole thing up himself.

I was disappointed. My short-lived dream of living for eternity on Earth Station, with Gwen by my side, had been dashed by her insatiable desire to experience things that would help her rekindle the feelings garnered by her former position of power. I tried to rationalize the whole thing by telling myself that everything happened for a reason and that Gwen would return quickly from the alien world, ready to settle down with me, my dogs, and One-eyed Jack. Alas, this hope was dashed as well.

"I want you to go with me," she said one morning as we lay together in bed after a night of furious love-making.

How could I say no?

*****

Of course, I couldn't say no. But the preparation process was hell on Earth Station. Most of it was easy, like the programming to get our minds acclimated to learning new languages, reading other minds, speaking telepathically, and enhanced strength and vision. All of those things had supposedly been part of my original programming, lost from the lightning strike, but I told the Teacher I wouldn't go through with that programming if there were any chance of losing my ability to talk with animals. He assured me that would be preserved, which ended up being the case.

We were told that even though the planet of Aria was only 11% larger than Earth, its gravity was 50% higher due to its composition of metals and minerals. Our enhanced strength would be enough to handle the additional gravity, but to make us more comfortable, we were also given a boost through some kind of medication. The Teacher said it would wear off relatively quickly, and by then, our bodies would have adapted to the new gravity anyway.

The Teacher taught us the Arian language. He knew it well, even though he admitted that he had never been in the same room with an Arian. Video communication was as close as he ever got to them. He told us that by using their language, we would ingratiate ourselves with them and be treated with more respect. Apparently, humans from the "Outer Worlds" were considered inferior. He told us to be gracious but careful and use our mind-reading capabilities as soon as possible to learn as much as we could. He seemed worried for us, but I wasn't sure why.

By far, the most grueling part of the reprogramming was the immortality treatments. They had been refined since Cynthia, Maddie, Gino, and the Teacher had gone through them, but they were no cakewalk. Gwen and I were quite ill during the treatments, and each died twice, only to be revived by that vat of golden liquid they put our bodies in. Ironically, the Teacher hadn't made the immortality treatment a requirement for our trip to Aria. It was Gwen who'd been adamant about it. She said that if she was going to leave Earth Station, she didn't want to give up her immortality by doing so, explaining that she loved being forty-eight, and if the opportunity was there to stay that age, she wanted to take it. And on top of that, she insisted I do it as well because she didn't want me any older than my fifty-three-year-old body was at that time. What Gwen wanted, she got. She and Maddie were very much alike in that way. And why should I refuse the opportunity to become immortal anyway?

We hadn't needed any of the unique stuff that Maddie had, like the ability to generate a force field or send a blast that could stun or kill an adversary or the Maker-ability of teleportation, and that's good because neither Gwen nor I wanted to be bald. Maddie was the most beautiful bald person I'd ever seen, but baldness wasn't for me. Gwen felt even more strongly about it.

The Teacher told us the Arians were peaceful people, yet they had defensive shields around their planet and the other planets in the solar system to thwart any alien attack that might come their way. They even had thousands of guard drones orbiting their sun to protect it from being destroyed by aggressors. The Teacher said several species in the galaxy could destroy a sun, including the Makers. But the Makers had made it known to all alien races that destroying suns and planets was prohibited and that severe consequences would ensue should that occur.

We all had been led to believe that the Makers were an observation-only species. Still, their actions on Earth and these other revelations about their cooperation with the Arians and threats toward violent races indicated otherwise. And our suspicions were confirmed when the Teacher revealed the underlying purpose of our visit from the Makers' perspective.

"There is something happening on Aria," he said. "Something the Makers don't understand and are being prevented from investigating."

"How can they prevent you from doing anything you want?" asked Gwen. "Can't you just beam down there or send Imprints to study the place like you do on Earth?"

"We cannot," he said. "Their energy shield blocks us from doing so."

"Can you at least see what's going on down there from space?" she asked.

"We can see, yes. But there are domes over certain areas. They are one of the things we are concerned about."

"Hmmm," she said. "Well then, why don't you just make a diplomatic visit, like the one we're going on?"

"Makers are not allowed on the planet," he said. "On the pretense that we cannot score high enough on their Human Purity scale."

"What's the Human Purity scale?" asked Gwen.

"It's a measurement criterion by which they rank the purity of humans. Since we are not human, we cannot pass the test."

"Are we going to be able to pass it?" she asked.

"I think so. Your manufactured bodies won't count against you; at least they won't disqualify you. And you both have other qualities that are valued on Aria."

"Such as?"

"It doesn't matter, Gwen. And frankly, the details of their test are not known to us. Perhaps we could figure out a way for Makers to pass it if they were. But neither of you are Makers and should be fine. You will either make it down to the planet's surface or not. If you fail the test, I will bring you back here."

"What is the secret you want us to look for there?" I asked.

"It's a suspicion, Zach, and by definition, if we don't know the secret, I can't tell you what to look for other than the domes, which may be completely irrelevant. But here's what we do know, all right?" Gwen and I nodded. "Every intelligent species in the Megaverse we have ever encountered has a life cycle. For many, it is brief. Environmental factors cause them to go extinct, or they destroy themselves or their planet, such as what Earth would likely have done had we not intervened. Some civilizations are destroyed by AI because they fail to properly manage the power of AI to learn. Left unchecked, AI will always destroy its creators. Luckily, most advanced societies realize this and take steps to limit AI's powers before it's too late.

"For those civilizations that make it through all of that and continue to advance, they inevitably reach a point where they become stagnant. No one needs to work because machines and AI are doing it all for them, and people simply get bored with their lives. The society becomes decadent and begins to decline, ultimately destroying itself."

"How long does this life cycle for advanced races usually last?" I asked.

"Normally, between ten and twenty thousand years after a species achieves light-speed travel, they fall into oblivion, with only scattered, ragged enclaves surviving."

"And how does this relate to the Arians?" asked Gwen.

"They achieved light speed capability fifty thousand years ago, yet continue to thrive. We don't know how."

Gwen raised her eyebrows. "Perhaps it's your cooperative program with them that's enabled them to thrive."

"That's quite possible," said the Teacher. "But we have no idea if that is true or not. Hopefully, you two can find out more."

*****

When the day finally arrived for us to leave, it was Earth Year 2044. I found it hard to believe that I'd been gone from Earth for five years, but the facts said otherwise. Anyway, our departure was celebrated at a party that was also a going away party for Maddie, Gino, and the twins. They were going to live on Earth so the twins could grow up, but they promised to return from time to time and to come back and live on Earth Station permanently when the twins were adults. Maddie honored me by asking if they could live in my home in the White Mountains, and I was happy to do that, especially since the house had been vacant for over six months. I told her to watch out for the timber rattlers with the twins (although they were pretty rare), but other than that, the animals in the forest liked humans.

"Keep an eye on Gwen," said Maddie, and I knew what she meant. Gwen was the firecracker of all firecrackers except for perhaps Maddie herself.

The party was only for our neighborhood, but there was one lady there whom I hadn't met yet. Her name was Jean Lemare. She was an attractive brunette who looked around sixty, and I was told she'd gone through the rebirth process, like Gwen, to make herself that age, which was the youngest she'd been when first marked by Maddie. They had a long history and seemed to care for each other deeply, and both of them shed tears when the goodbyes were said. Cynthia cried as well. The Teacher, well, you know the Teacher. I had some emotions when I said my goodbyes to my ten animals, but they seemed fine. They hung out with Cynthia more than they did with me, anyway. She must have spoiled them with treats, but it didn't matter. I felt comfortable leaving them with her on this beautiful little world I called home. I didn't plan on being gone that long anyway. I was sure Gwen would get bored on a peaceful planet like Aria and want to return to our solar system as soon as possible. Undoubtedly, my prediction of a rapid return to Earth Station after a brief and uneventful stay on Aria was the most significant miscalculation of my life.

PART TWO

Chapter 14

Aria/Earth Year 2044

It turns out that interstellar travel using the Pathways isn't exactly what I thought it would be. First, it's not the stars that are connected; it's certain planets in the solar systems. Usually, it's in the proximity of the largest planet where a Pathway terminates, and in our solar system, that planet was Jupiter. Another thing about the Pathways is that it's best, according to the Teacher, to use a spacecraft to transit through them.

When alone, the Teacher could bypass the Pathways and use his hive connections throughout the Megaverse to get from Point A to Point B. But he couldn't take a person with him using that method, except for "local" travel like going from Earth Station to Earth, or vice versa. As a result, we took a small vessel to Jupiter and used it to enter the Pathway System and then crisscross the galaxy until we arrived at the solar system where Aria was located.

It wasn't instantaneous. We had to endure hours passing through streaking lights that were the energy fields of the Pathways, and when we made a turn, we could feel it, just like making a turn while driving a car on a road. Well, not just like it, but the point is that you felt the turn, and it wasn't pleasant, as in my stomach was in knots. We eventually made it to the planet next door to Aria, the largest of five planets in that system, puttered over to Aria and established orbit around the planet. From my description, it may sound like it took days, weeks, or months to get there, but it was only around twelve hours in total, and most of that was getting to Jupiter. But definitely not instantaneous. I'd guess we were in the Pathways for at least a couple of hours.

The Teacher docked at some kind of space station that was orbiting the world of Aria. We weren't greeted by humans, robots, or anything with a physical body. Suddenly, a voice came out of the ceiling, but I saw no speakers or anything that might have been its source.

"Please follow the hallway to the Decontamination Center." The voice was pleasant. I couldn't tell if it was male or female. And it spoke English.

"I will leave you two here," said the Teacher. "Just let the Arians know when you want to leave, and they will contact me."

Gwen seemed concerned by this. "Are you sure we'll be all right?"

"Oh yes," he said. "I've been through the process up here before. The decontamination process is somewhat mundane, actually. Some kind of microscopic particle cleaning that you don't see, feel, or smell. They also check you for illness or disease during that procedure. Then they'll give you the Purity test, and if you pass, you will go to the surface."

"Can you wait until we at least see if we'll pass the test?" she asked. "I'll send you a thought message if we're all good."

"Very well," he said. "If it makes you feel better, I will stay a bit longer."

Gwen stepped forward and hugged the Teacher. "Thank you."

He smiled and gently pulled away from her. "You two will be fine."

I shook his hand. "Thank you, Teacher. We'll see you soon."

"Very well," he said.

We left him and followed the hallway to a doorway that opened upon our arrival. We entered a room that was empty, shaped like a cube, around ten feet on each side. The walls were a silvery metal material like the rest of the station.

"Hold your position for ten seconds, please," said the voice.

We stayed as we were and waited. I didn't see, hear, feel, or smell anything, as the Teacher had indicated would be the case.

"Please move through the doorway to the Testing Center."

A doorway slid open, and we carried on through it into another room that was larger than the Decontamination Center and dotted with small pedestals with screens on them.

"Each of you approach a testing unit, please."

Gwen stepped over to one of the units, and I did the same. I felt some kind of throbbing and looked up. I could see the shimmering energy of a force field surrounding me. I sent a thought to Gwen. *Are you okay?* She didn't look up from her console or respond, so I suppose the force field was blocking everything.

"Please look at the screen," came the voice.

I looked at the screen. A light flashed on, and I noticed it was covering my entire body.

"Please turn slowly in a circle."

I did as I was asked and, after a few seconds, faced the screen again.

"Category One score: Eleven. Please begin the next test. Recite these words with your best voice: You will obey."

I did as I was told. "You will obey."

"Category Two score: Nine. Please prepare for the next three tests. They will be conducted simultaneously. Close your eyes and hold very still."

I closed my eyes and waited. I didn't feel much, but I felt something. It was like receiving a thought transmission, but there were no words. Just a subtle feeling that something was going on in my brain that hadn't been going on before."

"Category Three score: Eighteen. Category Four score: Nine. Category Five score: Twelve. Total Human Purity score: Fifty-Nine. You are approved for travel to the surface of Aria. Please go through the opening and enter the Skytube."

The force field disappeared, a door opened, and I noticed Gwen was there at the opening waiting for me. "What was your score?" she asked.

"Fifty-nine. You?"

"Eighty-two," she said, and I could feel a swell of pride in her, based on the assumption that a higher score was better, which we knew was the case from what the Teacher had already told us. "You were approved for transit down to the surface, right?" she asked.

"Yes. Even though I am less pure than you, my queen."

She laughed at my joke. "Okay, good. I'll tell the Teacher we passed and let him know he can leave us now."

We stepped through the opening into a short tunnel, then through another portal into a tubular structure made entirely of glass. The only non-transparent part of the tube was the floor, which was made of the silvery metal. As soon as we got inside, the glass sealed up the opening, and the floor dropped slowly down, presumably taking us to the surface. It was a smooth transition from stationary to moving, but the speed of our descent gradually increased. Since we were in space, I could see other things in the distance. There were a few more stations, but only a limited number. I wondered if this was the only way people could get to the planet's surface.

The view of the planet itself was magnificent. It was mostly water, with many islands dotting its surface, although when I looked straight down, the land mass we were heading to didn't look very large. Overall, this planet reminded me very much of what I had always envisioned Earth Station to look like if you could have viewed it from space, and I wondered if the Makers had borrowed their design from this world.

There was cloud cover over much of the world, but I could see several other tubes traveling down to other islands. It looked like only one tube was going to each island, and I also saw a few islands with no tubes dedicated to them. I wondered if these were uninhabited or sparsely populated islands or if there was another reason there was no transit to and from space in those places. Then, on the distant horizon in what seemed to be an easterly direction, I saw one of the domes the Teacher had mentioned at the edge of my sightline. There was a tube going into the dome from space. The dome was black but didn't look solid, indicating that it might have been an energy field dedicated, at least in part, to visible obstruction. As we fell toward the surface, the dome disappeared over the horizon and out of my sight.

I saw no flying objects crisscrossing the skies and no boats of any kind on the open water. It was just the tube system I mentioned a moment ago that linked many of the islands together. The tubes were clear, like this one, although what was traveling inside the tubes was different from the simple platform in ours. They looked like cylinders, approximating the shape of a cork in a wine bottle, but of different lengths, I assumed to hold different numbers of passengers. There were two tubes per set, and the corks in the pairs were traveling in opposite directions. The tubes were arranged like a random set of spokes radiating out from the island directly below us, which wasn't large but seemed to be the central focus of the world below. The cork-shaped cylinders inside the tubes moved at very high speeds, almost too fast to see them go by. I tried to estimate how long it took for one of the corks to get from one island to the next, but it was impossible. Less than a second was all it took for a cork to make it across.

The island we were heading to spread out below us. While most of the other land masses had no tall buildings, this one seemed to be nothing but tall buildings, covering the entire island, beginning very close to the white sand beaches that composed the periphery and dominating the whole island. The buildings were of different heights, but all were made of the same silvery material as the space station, and all curved to a point at the top, like the top of a missile. I don't know what caused me to think this, but I wondered if these massive buildings, a few of which were well over three thousand feet tall, actually were missiles and could blast off into space whenever they wanted to. Not likely, but it's what crossed my mind at the time.

I noticed the platform beginning to decelerate, and after a few minutes, it came to rest in the center of a grand foyer inside one of those buildings I was describing. I could see through the clear tube that a crowd of around one hundred people were there. The thing is, these people were preposterously large. The men and women were all over seven feet tall, and the men were simply massive. Broad chests and heavily muscled arms and legs. The women were outrageously feminine, with the requisite shapes and curves one might associate with that. And all of them were bald and were wearing colorful, translucent garb, something like the ridiculous nightgowns the Teacher had made us wear, although much tighter to their bodies than ours. And while Gwen and I had insisted on wearing undergarments beneath our see-through clothes, these people had not elected that option. You can visualize what that means without me going into it here.

"Those guys could kill an ox with those tools," said Gwen, and I laughed. She could be hilarious when she wanted to be, especially when she felt the energy she so desperately craved, which seemed to be happening for her at that moment. And this was only the beginning because when the doors of our tube opened and we stepped out, the sound of what seemed like dozens of magnificent voices singing filled the air. And here's the thing. All of the singers were looking directly at Gwen.

Chapter 15

One

I had expected the visit of the Earthlings would be as devastatingly boring as colonial visits typically were, but the woman proved me wrong the moment she set foot on Aria. Her attendant was of no interest to anyone, but song erupted for her from more than a dozen members of the House of the One Hundred immediately upon her disembarkation from the Skytube. This had never happened before in my memory. Word had come down from the decontamination facility that her Purity score had registered within the Arian range, very rare for a colonist from any world, much less from a world that wasn't even halfway to their maturity goal. We hadn't expected to be seeing anyone from Earth for a thousand years, if ever, but here they were, courtesy of the Maker known as the Teacher.

Per Arian Law, the Teacher wasn't permitted on the planet's surface. Humans only, and while he occupied a facsimile of a human body (which we don't object to), that alone wouldn't do. He had to score at least fifty on the Human Purity scale, and his score never quite got there. As you would expect from an alien. I was surprised the woman's attendant scored as well as he did since he was in a poorly manufactured body, but he'd come up well above the range that humans from primitive planets were expected to achieve. 59. Not bad, although nearly half of it was his Raw Intelligence score, undoubtedly due to his programming when he was made. But it was enough to get him over the top. The woman, on the other hand, Gwendolyn Marks, was an anomaly that needed to be further studied.

I'd glanced at her Purity score when it was posted. An 82 on a scale where 100 was perfect. Most of the population on Aria scored lower than this and, as a result, received less income and privileges than those of us on the higher end of the range. No one works on Aria in the traditional sense. Some of us work hard to maximize our score, but that's by choice. A person can survive rather nicely even if they do nothing to improve their score. And let me be clear, when I say no one works on Aria, I'm speaking strictly about those of us who matter. There are islands, however, occupied exclusively by lower-class Arians, where people do work. They don't really have to since their government subsidy would be enough to survive on, even with their paltry

Purity scores, but they seem to actually enjoy it. Very hard to understand.

But I digress. Let's discuss the Human Purity score parameters in detail. There are five equally weighted categories, meaning a maximum score of 20 is possible in each. In the category of Physical Beauty, Gwendolyn Marks scored only 11. She was white, like us, but that didn't matter. The Physical Beauty category did not discriminate based on color, recognizing that it was only by chance that humans on Aria had evolved as white. The weather is mild here due to our position relative to our sun and its intensity, which is less than the intensity of the sun you call Sol. Our weather is also very stable since we have a circular orbit and virtually no tilt in our planet's axis relative to our sun. We are white because there was no need for our ancestors to produce extra melanin to protect their skin, as happened on worlds or regions of worlds where the sunlight is intense. But melanin content is a non-factor in our beauty scale. Height, bone structure, facial features, muscle tone, and the absence of hair are the main components of beauty for humans.

The scale calls for differences between males and females, particularly in bone structure and muscle tone. Males are expected to be more massive, and they are, but no taller than females. Compared to humans from other worlds, our men are giants. Well-sculpted giants and much larger than males from the colonies. Our women are simply taller. And while their breasts are no longer needed for child-rearing, they are still valued as part of the equation of beauty, so they have them.

Gwendolyn's weaknesses in the Physical Beauty category were her height and her hair. To give you some perspective, I am 229 of your centimeters tall. In your Imperial system, that is seven feet six inches. This woman was just under six feet tall. Very short. Very low class. We couldn't make her taller unless we made her a new body (which we had no intention of doing), but if she had agreed to take the hair-cleansing solution, she could have raised her score by 5 points. There were people on Aria who had hair, but these were the lower classes, those who had given up on becoming pure generations ago.

Again I digress. We have four more categories to discuss, so I must move on. In the category of Voice Command, Gwendolyn scored 17, even though she refused to sing. Most of us sang when we took that test and practiced for hours each day preceding the annual Purity Census. But she was obviously a person who was born to command others. Hadn't she been some kind of leader back on Earth? I couldn't remember.

Her score in the Raw Intelligence category was 18, a formidable number, but easily duplicated or exceeded through AI infusions. But the score which had everyone stirred up was her result in the Ambition category, a 19 out of a possible 20. And while each category was weighted equally with the others, there was a bit of cult magic surrounding Ambition here on Aria because it was sorely lacking in most of the population. My score of 19 was the highest Ambition score recorded in the last 100 Revs. For an off-worlder to score this high was rare indeed. And she had nearly equaled that with her score in Category Five, Ingenuity.

An 18 was a higher Ingenuity score than virtually all of the people here in the House of the One Hundred and, once again, equal to my own. Her total score of 82 would put her in the top 100,000 on the planet, and while it was nowhere close to my best total score of 97 (from the most recent census), it wasn't the total that was intriguing to those of us who were in the know, so to speak. An Earthling receiving a 19 on Ambition and an 18 on Ingenuity was a valuable commodity here on Aria. Altogether unexpected and exceedingly alluring. Based on those scores, she was unlikely to ever leave this planet. In fact, I intended to make sure of that.

Obviously, serval of my colleagues wanted to jump right in and couple with her, hence the singing. She wouldn't know that we sing when we want to couple. I planned on explaining it to her during our private audience unless her guide had already covered it. The guide would likely do that and might even go through the obligatory introductions to her suitors in the hope that she might accept one of them. I would enjoy coupling with her myself to gain firsthand knowledge of the source of her exceptional category scores. Coupling was the best way to get into a person's Essence, other than the machines the Makers had provided. But not everyone had access to these devices, hence the singing of my colleagues to attract her to them. From a practical point of view, the woman was too small for a male Arian to couple with, which explained why only females had been signing. I am male; thus, I would be precluded from coupling with the woman for purely practical reasons. We try not to harm our guests, after all.

In case you wondered, my current Arian name is best translated as "One" since, at the moment, I register higher on the Purity scale than anyone on Aria and, therefore, higher than any human in the universe. I've been in the Ten for as long as I can remember and have been "One" for serval Revs. One Rev, the time it takes Aria to circle our sun, is about half an Earth Year. No one kept the number one ranking for more than a few Revs, but while you did, you were the de facto leader of our world and showered with riches and privileges. The downside was hosting meetings like this one, although the woman might add a little spice to the drudgery.

The Earthlings were inappropriately dressed, a typical mistake for colonials. They wore translucent garb, as all of us do here, for comfort and to display what lies underneath. Still, their dress style was too loosely fitting for daytime apparel and more appropriate for use in the confines of one's residence or before coupling because the loose attire was easy to remove. And they had, for some reason, worn undergarments, also a big no-no.

Oh, by the way, our days are very long here due to the slow rotation of our planet. A day here lasts for nearly one of your months, half light and half dark. But we don't change our clothes based on light or dark. We don't sleep, so our clothing choice is primarily based on whether we are in public or in private. And since I would be meeting with the Earthlings, I had donned the tighter fabric. I wondered if what showed beneath would frighten the woman, as so often happened when primitives from the outer worlds visited their Creators. I hoped it did, because she very much needed to be afraid of me.

Chapter 16

Immediately upon disembarking from the tube, we were met by a woman who looked like the rest of them. She was radically tall but with graceful female curves and intense, sparkling green eyes, and was dressed in a multi-colored, tightly-fitting translucent gown. A breathtaking woman with every aspect of her beauty on display.

"Welcome," she said in English. "I am called One Hundred and will be your guide."

Gwen extended her hand to shake, but the woman did not reciprocate.

"That is not one of our customs here," she said. "We are aware of it, but it is not something we do."

Gwen tilted her head to the side, and I wondered if she would say something aggressive, but she didn't. "We can speak your language if you want us to," said Gwen. "We'd prefer it, so we can practice."

I saw the skin above the woman's eyes move, the place where her eyebrows would have been if she had them. "Very well." She turned to the crowd, who had finally stopped signing. "Will the singers come forward, please?"

I counted fourteen of the females that had stepped out of the crowd and gathered in a semi-circle in front of us. She introduced them one at a time. "This is Three, this is Seven, this is Nine…" I think you get the picture. They all had numbers for names. And she introduced them in ascending order. The last of them was called Fifty-three. I noticed that all the numbers were much lower than our guide's number, who you may remember was named "One Hundred."

"What is the significance of the numbers?" I asked.

"We are the one hundred highest-ranked humans on Aria," she said. "For this Rev, we will live here in the House of the One Hundred."

It didn't take a brain surgeon to figure out that our guide was the lowest-ranked human in the House of the One Hundred and had been given Guide-duty, no doubt a less than prestigious assignment.

"What's a Rev?" asked Gwen.

"It is the time it takes our planet to circle our sun. In your language, it is called a Year. One Rev is about half of one of your years. Each new Rev, a new Purity Census is taken, and that Rev's One Hundred are chosen."

"What do you people do here?" asked Gwen.

"We do whatever we like," said One Hundred, smiling. "Now, have you made your selection Gwendolyn?"

"I'm not sure what you mean," said Gwen.

"You have not been briefed on our customs? This is highly irregular."

"We have no one to brief us since you won't allow the Makers on your planet. They don't know anything about your customs as far as I've heard."

"That is not true," said One Hundred. "But it doesn't matter. I will explain this custom to you. When a person sings to another on Aria, it is an expression of affection. And a request to spend time with you as your partner."

Gwen frowned at this revelation and took my hand. "Zach, here is my partner, so I'm sorry to say I'm already spoken for."

"Oh, I see," said One Hundred. "That is unfortunate. Staying with one partner for an extended time is not done here. But if it is your custom, we must respect that."

"Yes, it's our custom," said Gwen, looking up at her fourteen suitors. "Thank you all very much. I am honored by your, uh, affection for me."

The fourteen bowed and turned back to the crowd, most shaking their heads, seemingly frustrated they hadn't been selected.

"Now I will take you to an audience with One," said One Hundred. "And then I will show you where you will stay. Please, follow me."

*****

One Hundred led us to a lift that took us high up into the building. When we disembarked, it was obvious that we had been taken to the structure's apex, as the shape of the vast circular chamber we entered curved up to the tip, as in the form of a missile I had described earlier. It was also clear that this was the tallest building in the city because every square inch of the outside walls was clear as glass. Since the outside of all the buildings had appeared as silvery metal, these structures were likely built as vast one-way mirrors. People could see out but not in.

In the center of the room was a circle of comfortable-looking chairs, and from one of them rose a massive creature. Male, with a broad chest and rippled muscles, around seven and a half feet tall, and entirely without hair. The features of his face were exceedingly well-defined and perfect, even from the point of view of someone from another planet like me. He was human, after all, although I must admit that if someone had told me he wasn't, I wouldn't have argued. His appearance wasn't what one would expect the evolution of the human race to lead to. I don't know why I thought this, but this man seemed not very human at all to me, even though he was supposedly the most perfect human in the universe.

"May I introduce One," said One Hundred, continuing to use Arian.

The giant smiled and approached, looming over us like a lion over a hyena he was about to devour. We knew well enough not to offer our hands to shake, and when I observed him give a slight bow with his enormous head, I did the same, and so did Gwen.

"Welcome to Aria," he said, his voice the deep bass one might expect. But it also contained some other quality, something that made me want to hear more. Frankly, I was utterly riveted by his voice. If, in his following words, he had told me to jump out of a window, I believe I would have seriously considered it.

"Thank you," said Gwen, taking the lead as always. "It seems to be an extraordinary place."

"We like to think so," he said. "Please, come sit with me." He turned and walked lightly toward the group of chairs, and I noticed he wore no shoes. I turned back and looked at the feet of One Hundred, and they were also bare. "Are you thirsty or hungry?" he asked, taking a seat.

Gwen answered for both of us. "We are thirsty and hungry, but we know nothing about what you drink or eat here, so we don't know what to ask for."

"One Hundred has been studying your culture and has asked the Kitchen to prepare some hor d'oeuvres and refreshments you will be familiar with. I look forward to trying some of them myself."

I glanced over at One Hundred and saw her approaching a silvery tube that had sprouted from the floor. On top of it was a tray of appetizers, bottles of red and white wine, and a water pitcher. No beer, unfortunately. One Hundred approached the tray but didn't pick it up. Instead, it rose from the tube and floated beside her as she approached us. A circular table of the same silvery material rose from the floor between our chairs, and the tray settled onto it. One Hundred took a seat next to One.

"Red or white wine?" she asked. "Water, perhaps?"

"White wine for me, thank you," said Gwen.

"I'll have some water, thank you," I said.

I wasn't surprised to see the wine and water pour themselves and come to us. It appeared that these humans had mastered levitation, or perhaps some other technological trick was playing out. We both took hold of our glasses and drank.

"Excellent wine," said Gwen smiling.

"Would you like to try some food?" asked One Hundred.

I glanced at the tray and saw a shrimp cocktail, mushroom caps stuffed with crab, and cheese and crackers. My stomach growled. "I would be happy to try a little of everything," I said.

The food I had asked for rose and settled onto a plate, which came toward me, along with a napkin. I tried to wait a few seconds before eating but was so hungry that I couldn't. I snatched a shrimp, dabbed it into the cocktail sauce on my plate, and munched on it. Exquisite. The best shrimp I had ever tasted.

"If I may," said Gwen, "I'd like to ask about that Human Purity test we took on the station up above. What is its purpose?"

"It tells us how human you are," said One.

"Yes, of course," she said. "But five categories are used to compile your total score. Can you explain them to me?"

One reached for a mushroom cap and placed it in his cavernous mouth. "Hmmm, these are good. But I'm sorry to report that we cannot provide further details of the Purity test. Suffice it to say that you have passed the test, which suggests your planet is developing nicely."

"But One," said Gwen, not giving up. "We are your progeny, from what I'm told. Your children. Why wouldn't you want to teach us all you can about who we are?"

One smiled and shook his head. "Oh, but we do, Gwendolyn. We so very much want you to learn as much as we can convey. But Human Purity must be attained by yourselves, just as we did. The struggle to ascend goes a long way to defining what being human is. Independence, ingenuity in the face of adversity, and the will to carry on no matter what obstacles present themselves. This process will help your people more than we ever could."

Gwen seemed unhappy that One was withholding what appeared to be basic information about Aria and humans in general. I could tell she was about to say something she might regret. *Stay calm*, I said to her mind. She relented and fell back into her chair.

"Please tell us about your planet if it is allowed," I said. "It seems to be mostly islands. And I saw that some of them are connected by tubes like the one we traveled on to the surface. Is that the primary mode of transportation here? By these tubes?"

"Yes, it is," he said. "First, I should explain that we don't travel much from place to place here on our planet. Our focus is on interstellar travel, exploring the universe. Our planet is wonderful, but once you've seen one island, you've essentially seen them all."

"This island seems different than the others I saw from the tube from space. It's full of these exceptionally tall buildings, whereas the others seemed less developed."

"Yes, this island is the capital of our world," he said. "By the way, the closest English translation of our city's name is First Eden, which you may recognize from your bible."

"Are you religious?" I asked.

"Yes and no," he said. "Yes, in that we believe there are superior beings. No, in that we don't worship a deity. The name is simply meant to commemorate the place where human life first evolved, which we know to be here, on this island."

"How do you know that?" I asked.

"Not important," he said.

I was taken aback by his abrupt ending to that line of conversation, so I decided to get back on track regarding more practical matters. "I noticed some of the islands weren't connected by either kind of tubes. Neither the ones from space nor the ones over the water. Are they uninhabited?"

"No, all the islands of Aria support human life," he said. "Some of them are the homes of lesser humans, however, and these people are not permitted to travel, either around Aria or into the heavens. We cannot allow those who refuse to improve themselves to infect the rest of us. They in no way resemble what an Arian truly is. We tolerate them but don't condone or reward their ambivalence."

I felt as if I was getting somewhere in terms of learning things about Aria that the Teacher didn't know. The place was obviously not a utopia if they discriminated against and imprisoned some of their own people. I also assumed that while I was carrying the conversation that Gwen was reading One's mind to learn more, but I was emboldened to carry on with my spoken inquires.

"What about the black dome I saw on the horizon during our descent from space? What kind of place is that?"

One yawned as if becoming bored with us. He stood, completely ignoring my question. "It was a pleasure to meet you both," he said. "I hope you enjoy your time on Aria."

One Hundred stood, and so did we, having been dismissed. "Thank you for your time," I said. Gwen remained mute, finishing her wine, then glaring at the being in front of us, known here on Aira as the most perfect human in the universe. I wondered what that really meant.

As we turned to leave, One provided some ominous advice. "I should warn you that mind-reading is frowned upon on Aria. You won't be imprisoned if you continue to use it, but you will be deported. It doesn't work on Arians, anyway. Our minds are too powerful to be read."

With the giant's last words simmering in our minds, we bowed in his direction, turned, and followed One Hundred out of the chamber.

Chapter 17

One Hundred took us to a nearby building made of the same one-way mirror substance as all the others but not nearly as tall as the one where the one hundred purest humans lived. I wondered why they needed such a gigantic structure for only a hundred people. It was more than three thousand feet tall and could easily accommodate thirty thousand residents if it were a high rise in an Earth-based city. I tried to imagine what they did with all of that space. They must have had gymnasiums, sports centers, entertainment venues, restaurants, and probably even amusement parks that catered to the whims of the one hundred inhabitants. But I would never know because we were shown nothing of that place on our first day or our last.

Before our trip to Aria, we had asked the Teacher if we needed to pack clothing and toiletries, and he said he had been told those wouldn't be required. And when we entered the vast apartment we would share, I found out why. One Hundred showed us closets filled with clothes, and there was a kitchen area (which wasn't really a kitchen because all the food was already prepared) filled with culinary delights, most of Earthly inspiration, like the appetizers we had enjoyed during our meeting with One.

When I inquired about toiletries, One Hundred took us into the bedroom, which was immense and contained a circular bed the diameter of a small Ferris wheel, beside which was a room with a toilet but no sink, shower or tub. And no toilet paper, either. The toilet itself was also unique in that it had no lids. It was simply a molded bowl with a comfortable seat that was part of its structure. I wondered how that could be sanitary.

My confusion was ended by One Hundred's explanation. "You may deposit your waste here," she said, pointing at the toilet. "It is always best to come into this room unclothed because it will clean whatever needs cleaning on your body, including after your waste disposal. Our garb is designed for easy removal for that very practical reason. The decorative aspects of the clothing are for aesthetic as opposed to functional purposes. There is no need to give the room detailed instructions. Just say the word 'clean.' If your teeth and mouth need cleaning, the room will open and clean your mouth. If your body contains too much residue from perspiration, it will cleanse it away. And the remains of your waste will, of course, be removed, including any residual odors. The disposal unit itself will also be hygienically purified."

"Does it do it with water?" I asked.

"No, Zachary, it does not. It is a process similar to the decontamination process you experienced up above. You won't feel it, but it will happen. Trust me."

"What's on the agenda for the rest of the day?" asked Gwen.

"Day is a word we do not use here," said One Hundred. "Our planet rotates very slowly. It takes around thirty of your days for a full Rote, so any given spot on the planet receives light continuously for around half of that time and then is dark during the other half. Daylight has been with us for eight of your days during this Rote, so there should be plenty of sunshine for the remainder of your stay."

I wondered what led this woman to believe that a five or six-day visit would satisfy Gwen, but I hoped she was right. I was homesick for my animals already and felt distinctly uneasy in this place. I wanted to go home but needed to make the best of things while we were here.

"Which direction does the sun rise in?" I asked.

"The sun rises in the east," she said, pointing in what must have been an easterly direction.

"So when the sun sets in the west, the darkness comes from the East?"

"Yes, of course. Why is that important to you?"

"No reason," I said, but I was thinking that if we somehow found a way to get to the East, which was the direction of the dome, it might be dark there soon. Which was good for us because the cover of darkness was always good when you're sneaking around, right? And we see very well at night, so perhaps we could learn something of value when night arrived.

"How do you structure your life, then, between times of darkness and times of light?" asked Gwen.

"Our life does not change when it is dark since our eyes see very well at night." Well, so much for that advantage. "For you, it might be more challenging since I believe it is always light at the station where you live. Did you know we built that station?"

"Yes, we were told you build all the stations for the Makers," said Gwen.

"All of the ones needed in the Milky Way, Canus Major Dwarf, and Draco II galaxies," she replied. "They work with other vendors in galaxies and universes elsewhere. You see, the Makers need partners in the physical world, and they have awarded us the contract for the three galaxies I mentioned."

"What do you get in return?" asked Gwen.

"Knowledge. Technology. For example, we travel on the interstellar Pathways shown to us by the Makers. And we have been given their Essence harvesting and body reengineering technology. That is why you will see no children here on Aria. We just remake ourselves when the time comes for that."

"Interesting," said Gwen, strolling over to the kitchen and pouring herself a glass of wine. "But circling back, how do you organize your time here?"

"Each individual is free to use their time as they choose. We typically are awake for around twenty of your hours and sleep for around ten. My time for sleeping is coming soon, so I must leave you, but I will return after that and show you around our magnificent city if you would like."

"Are we free to move around the city ourselves?" asked Gwen.

One Hundred hesitated but quickly recovered. "Why, yes." She reached into her clothing and withdrew two wristbands made from the silvery material as most things on Aria seemed to be made. "These are money repositories," she said. "You can use them to buy material things and services, such as transportation and dining."

We both slipped the bands onto our wrists. "Can we ride the tubes to the other islands?" I asked.

Again, a slight pause. "I believe there is enough money on these wristbands to get you to and from the nearest island, but the tubes are mainly for moving supplies and provisions, not people. People have no ongoing need to travel from island to island here. But when they do, it is quite expensive."

"Hmmm," said Gwen. "Well, I'm sure we'll be busy just getting to know First Eden. How many people live here in the city, by the way?"

"Ten million exactly," said One Hundred. "The ten million that rank highest on the Purity scale. The others live on other islands."

"What is the population of the planet?" asked Gwen.

"One billion," said One Hundred.

"Exactly?" asked Gwen.

"Yes, exactly. That is the limit for sustaining perfect harmony on our world."

"It seems your system is highly efficient," said Gwen. "No need for elections to determine who is in charge. Social status is clearly defined. And everyone has exactly what they need and what they deserve."

"I couldn't have said it better myself," said One Hundred. "I will leave you then for my sleep and return in ten of your hours."

One Hundred left us alone.

"Seems we have a lot to talk about," said Gwen.

Yes, but I think we should speak this way, don't you? I asked.

Absolutely.

*****

One Hundred was a newcomer to the elite of the elite, having worked for generations to earn her way to the top. Her recent Purity score of 87 was impressive, especially since she showed great promise of continued improvement. But she had a lot to learn about how to manage unruly guests. Thus I had demanded that she return to me at her earliest convenience. Apparently, she had lied to them about needing sleep to get back to me as soon as possible.

"Did they try to read your mind?" I asked.

"Not after you warned them, One," she said.

"They ask too many questions," I said. "I am considering deporting them immediately."

I had not felt fury like this in many Revs and never concerning outsiders. They were always dull, but not these two renegades.

"Of course, that is your decision," said One Hundred. "But we must consider the ramifications with the Makers if we do so. Perhaps we should give it a bit longer and let them tire of being here on their own. After all, they will see nothing of importance."

"Is it their intent to go exploring on their own?"

"I believe it is One, but they can't get far with the credits we provided. And the wristbands are also tracking beacons, so we will always know where they are."

"I will leave it to you to track them, then," he said. "And I want to know if anything out of the ordinary occurs. Is that understood, One Hundred?"

"Without question, One. It will be done."

I was impressed by One Hundred's submissiveness. It was a good sign that she understood the House of the One Hundred pecking order. If I am honest, it aroused me, perhaps because I was agitated.

"How long did you tell them you would sleep?" I asked.

"Ten Hours." She had a smile on her face as if she'd guessed my next question.

"Would you like to spend some time with me in my private entertainment center, One Hundred? We can watch a feed from Earth. One that puts us in the right mood."

"I WOULD BE HONORED!" she sang, in full-throated harmony with my own desires.

Chapter 18

I'm pretty keyed up, said Gwen. *You?*

Yeah, but this place is weird. Don't you think?

Absolutely, but that's probably why we're so excited, right? She smiled. *You feel like burning off some excess energy before we investigate further?*

Good thinking, I said, winking.

It was true that both of us were wound up tight after our first few hours on Aria. Yes, there was a big mystery brewing as to what the heck was going on there, but it was still exciting. Exhilarating, really, and it produced the same urge in both of us. I'm not sure all humans reacted this way to tenuous circumstances, but Gwen and I certainly did. We stripped out of our clothes and jumped into the oversized circular bed. I suppose you could call it a "Triple King" if such as classification exists. There were no sheets or blankets on the bed, and those definitely weren't needed at the moment, but I did enjoy sleeping with sheets and a blanket and briefly wondered where those would come from or if they simply weren't part of "Arian Culture." However, the absence of those familiar bedtime accouterments was of no concern to us right then and there.

We attacked each other, which was turning into our "go-to" approach to lovemaking. Something about us as a couple brought out the animal in us. We enjoyed each other for over an hour, a short stint compared to normal, but we had work to do. When we'd finished, I nestled up to Gwen and asked her a question. I don't know if it was the release from our sexual encounter and the carefree state of mind that tends to come with it, but I used my spoken voice, and so did she.

"What did you feel when those Arian females sang to you?" I asked. "Especially after you found out what it meant?"

Gwen sat up in bed and gazed at me. Despite being absolutely satisfied sexually, I couldn't help but feel a tinge of awe at Gwen's beauty and her lack of shyness in displaying it, at least to me. And if you think about it, with no sheets or blankets on the bed, what choice did she have?

"Do I detect a slight pulse of jealousy from you, Zachary Hurts?"

I smiled. "Absolutely not, Gwendolyn Marks. If we never again came together in the way we just experienced, I would still be grateful for all that we have shared. I mean it, Gwen. Being with you has been the honor of my life, and I still wonder how it happened."

She shook her head. "Thank you, Zach. I'm touched. But it sounds like you wanted to be with me because I used to be the President. I'd rather you just liked me for who I am, not who I was."

"I *love* you for who you are," I countered. "The thing that made you President, that zest for attaining the unobtainable, is what I love. It doesn't come to me naturally, but it's there when I'm with you."

"That sounds better! And you've got nothing to worry about. I'm not about to abandon you for some seven-foot-tall sexual sideshow. But if you want the truth, I was attracted to those women, but that doesn't mean I'm going to jump into bed with them. They all looked identical to me, although I was definitely drawn to them. I have no idea why. Let me tell you a story, okay?"

"Certainly."

"Back when I was in college, in a psychology class, we were told to review a study conducted by some prestigious research university on the sexual proclivities of both men and women. A large group of self-identified heterosexual men were in one group, and a large group of self-identified heterosexual women were in the other. In private, individual sessions, the men were shown pictures of naked men, some of them portraying men with men, and then were asked to fill out a questionnaire regarding their reaction to these pictures. The women underwent the same process; only the pictures were of women. Please also note that they were given legal documents guaranteeing anonymity. Plus, they were being paid, which can sometimes 'guilt' people into telling the truth. I'm sure some respondents were untruthful, but do you care to guess what the overall results indicated?"

"I dare not even guess," I said.

"The overwhelming majority of the men responded that they were not sexually aroused by the pictures, and most indicated they were appalled by them. The majority of women, however, responded that they were aroused, at some level, by what they had seen, and only small numbers were appalled."

"And your conclusions?" I asked.

"I thought my professor, who was a woman, by the way, said it best. 'Most women are a little bit gay.'"

"And you feel you fall into that category, I take it?"

"I know I do," she said.

"Have you ever been with a woman?"

"I have not," she said. "But I am attracted to women. One in particular."

"Maddie," I said. "Right?"

"Is it that obvious?" she asked.

"It is to me, Gwen. And it doesn't bother me because I have the same attraction to her. I think everyone who meets her does. Do you mind me asking if Maddie knows about your feelings for her?"

"Maddie and I have never discussed it in detail," said Gwen. "And it doesn't matter because she's fully committed to Gino. I would never interfere with that. She can't get to the part of my mind where that secret is hidden anyway, so even though she may suspect I'm attracted to her, she can't know for sure. I seem to have some special ability to block my most personal feelings from anyone."

"Like the Arians!" I said. "Except they can block everything. Maybe that's why you scored so high on the test!"

"Maybe so. Hey, why don't we get cleaned up and figure out what to do next, okay?"

"You got it! And Gwen, thanks for your honesty. It's a real turn-on."

"Another round then before we "cleanse?""

"As you command, my lady."

*****

We took turns in the cleansing room, putting on new clothing, deciding to forgo our underwear and jump headfirst into the Arian culture. After that, we ate a massive meal in our kitchen. I'm sorry to report they didn't have steak, but there was some delicious salmon and an array of cooked vegetables. I piled my plate with asparagus and red potatoes, slathered some butter on both, and found dill sauce for the fish. It was delicious, and I wondered how they kept it all tender and just the right temperature. Gwen wasn't a strict vegetarian (although, by definition, all of us living on Earth Station were pescatarians), but she decided against meat and stuffed herself with pasta and veggies, topped off with wine that she said was quite tasty. I stuck with iced tea.

We found some nifty backpacks in the closet and stuffed them with extra food, water, and clothes. I call them nifty because the straps were nearly invisible, and when we put them on, the packs themselves faded out of sight, all supposedly to allow us to display ourselves properly while in public, I guessed.

Our conversation about what to do next was brief because we both wanted to do the same thing. We assumed we'd be given very little access to anything of interest here in First Eden since we'd been shown virtually nothing in the House of the One Hundred, which was large enough to have kept us busy for weeks exploring its secrets. But that wasn't going to happen, and we figured that without a guide, we'd have even less of a chance of accessing anything interesting here in First Eden. Our plan was simply to take a tube to a nearby island and see if we could find a way of getting even further. The idea was that the more distance we put between ourselves and First Eden, the more freedom we would have to find something of interest. The food and the extra change of clothes were there to help us keep going for as long as we could and to save money, which both of us suspected had been allocated to us in a limited supply to curtail our curiosity.

Neither of us had believed One Hundred's story about needing sleep because we both inhabited engineered bodies, just as she did, and we didn't need sleep at all, although both Gwen and I slept some each night, more out of habit than anything else. We figured she'd gone to get further instructions on what to do with us from One and would be returning to watch over us soon. We left the apartment and had no trouble using the elevator to get to the ground floor. While mind-reading might be illegal for humans, our guess was that the AI running the elevator had done just that because neither of us had said a word or pushed the button. Who knows. This was a very strange place and not so easy to figure out. Nevertheless, as we emerged onto the streets of First Eden, I felt a sense of adventure tingling in my gut, and when I looked at Gwen, I saw the energy in her eyes. I didn't know what was ahead of us, but it made me happy to see Gwen thriving, something she'd been struggling with after her two terms as President of the United States had ended.

The streets were surprisingly empty for a city of ten million people. There were no vehicles. People were getting around using their legs and nothing else. We attracted quite a few stares since we were much shorter than all of them and had hair. And while I would have expected their gazes to include expressions of disdain due to our inherent and obvious "inferiority," instead, we received welcoming smiles that seemed to suggest an awareness that we were guests from another world. Regardless of the reason, it was reassuring and gave us a much-needed dose of confidence as we pressed forward.

When I looked up into the sky, I became disoriented by the sheer height of the buildings. I could barely see the top of the House of the One Hundred, but the lesser buildings (none shorter than a thousand feet by my estimation) all displayed the missile-like shape I'd observed during our descent from space on the tube. Again, I wondered if these buildings could actually fly if they needed to, but for the life of me, I couldn't imagine why they would need to do that.

The streets were paved in silver, if you will. The same silvery substance that everything else was made of, but it wasn't slippery on the feet. We had on our shoes, but it was becoming increasingly apparent that they made us look foolish in the eyes of the natives, none of whom wore them.

"Do you think we should ditch the shoes?" I asked Gwen.

"Why?" she asked.

"To help us fit in, maybe."

"We'll never fit in here unless we shave our heads and grow a few feet taller. I like my shoes. Fuck 'em if they can't take a joke."

Getting a wake-up call from Gwen when you needed one was always helpful.

The city wasn't significant in terms of area, as one might think a city of ten million would be. I guessed that was because each building held so many people, except for the sparsely populated House of the One Hundred. The entire island was around the size of Central Park in New York, which wasn't small by any means at 843 acres. Still, even that represented only six percent of the total area of Manhattan, which had a similar population to First Eden. At any rate, my point here is that we made it to the island's edge relatively quickly and found the tube station without any trouble.

There were no attendants at the station, which wasn't a surprise. We were on a platform, and I saw a spot where boarding could occur. I looked down the platform towards the city and saw both the incoming and outgoing tubes curled under the platform there. A machine with numerous appendages was working there, perhaps executing some repair or maintenance procedure. I imagined that all the work that kept this city running was taking place underneath the floor of the city. Machines like that one or a similar design probably performed all the tasks needed. Loading and unloading, sorting the merchandise, and moving it to its ultimate destination. It had to be that way because there was no work going on above ground from what we had seen on our way here.

We had the wristbands but saw nowhere to use them.

"They'll probably just deduct our fare automatically," said Gwen. "Let's try to get on one of these things."

It was obvious that all the cylinders coming into New Eden were full of goods while all of them going out were empty, meaning that nothing was produced here in the central city, and it would be easy to catch a ride to the next island, as long as we could figure out how to do it. There were no signs telling us what the next island's name was or anything to tell us how to get on, so we just stood on the platform and waited. A small cylinder stopped in front of us, and a doorway appeared. We stepped on. The doorway closed. There were no seats, and no straps were hanging from the ceiling to steady us, but just before the cylinder launched, I felt my feet gripped by the floor as a piece of steel would be grabbed by a magnet. We shot off at a tremendous rate of speed, but neither of us lost our balance, somehow held vertically by forces within the tube. Within seconds, we had arrived.

Chapter 19

We emerged from the tube and stepped onto the platform of the new island, name unknown. I glanced back to where we had come from, and even though First Eden was a long way away, it still dominated the skyline. I envisioned the Emerald City in the ever-popular Wizard of Oz, but on steroids that had caused it to sprout into the sky in a display of majesty unlike any I had seen before. I breathed deeply, and the air felt crisp and clean, tinged with a slight smell of salt from the ocean surrounding us.

We left the platform and walked into the city. The island was all city, just as First Eden was, although the buildings here were less magnificent than those of First Eden. Still made from the same silvery one-way mirror material but far shorter and blockier in design. There was a little flare—a curve here, a sharp angle there—but it was a step down without question. The people looked essentially the same as those we had seen in First Eden. Tall, the men massive, the women shapely. A few we saw were under seven feet tall, but everyone was hairless, the norm here, it seemed. The other thing I noticed was that we received less smiles from people as we passed. Looks of disdain and disgust were our greeting here.

"What do you think that's all about?" I asked Gwen, and she knew exactly what I was referring to.

"These people are second-class citizens, and they know it," she said. "I would imagine they have some resentment built up about that, so when they see 'inferiors' like us, they react by letting us know that we are inferior, and that makes them feel a little better about themselves. That's what I think, anyway."

"I wonder if that will get worse if we make it to another island, further out," I said.

"My bet would be yes. Let's try to find out, okay?"

We traversed the city in about twenty minutes, passing over canals that seemed to crisscross the island. We saw small boats motoring quietly along the canals, the first boats I had seen in this ocean world. The people riding the boats were Arians, and they were recreating, i.e., trying to enjoy themselves with a little boat ride, maybe a visit to a friend or some such thing. It was the first sign of anything remotely similar to the ways of Earth and Earth Station, so I suppose I felt a glimmer of hope that perhaps this entire world wouldn't be so sterile. So secretive.

We made it to the tube station on the other side of the island and observed three pairs of tubes pointing outward. The center tube departed the island at a ninety-degree angle, and the other two were at forty-five-degree angles. I looked out into the ocean to see where each of them led. The two angled lines terminated at islands I could see in the distance, while the one that went straight out traveled over the horizon without an endpoint in sight.

"Let's take the longest one," said Gwen.

We stepped up to the entry area, and an empty cylinder stopped in front of us. The door opened, and we stepped on. The door closed, and we shot off toward our unseen destination, somewhere out there. This trip took noticeably longer than the first one, lasting at least ten seconds, which meant we had traveled a long way. How far was unknown, but when we stepped off and looked back, the skyline of First Eden was nowhere to be seen.

"To the next tube station?" I asked Gwen.

"Why not," she said.

We passed across the island, and I noticed it wasn't completely covered with buildings. Green areas looked like parks, and people were lounging there in the sun. The buildings we saw seemed mainly industrial, like factories, processing plants, or warehouses. There were a few blocky apartment complexes, but it was obvious that the population here had even less status than what we had seen on the last island. The people were noticeably shorter than they were on the two islands we'd just been on, although quite a bit taller than us. A few of them even had hair. Short and neatly trimmed, but still, hair.

A pattern was emerging that the further we got from First Eden, the less "pure" the people became. Unfortunately, their lack of purity, i.e., their similarity to us, didn't correspond with their reaction upon seeing us, which was more hostile than we had encountered even on the last island. A few yelled words we didn't recognize, probably obscenities we hadn't been taught when we learned the language. We rushed across the island as fast as we could, crossing over a few bridges that spanned the canals and ultimately arriving at the tube station. This station had six pairs of tubes, fanning out as a hand of cards might in a game of Rummy.

"Which one?" I asked, having observed that none of the six traveled to a destination that could be seen with the naked eye.

"Do you remember where that black dome on the horizon was when we saw it from space? Did it seem directly east of First Eden, or was it more northerly or southerly?"

"Definitely more to the north," I said.

"Let's try the one on the left," said Gwen.

We approached the entry area and waited for a cylinder to arrive. After five minutes, we concluded that the cylinder wasn't coming because the AI sensors that collected the money had detected that we didn't have an adequate fare to pay for the transit.

"Let's try the next one over," said Gwen.

We did that and struck paydirt. A cylinder arrived, the door opened, and we stepped on. After another ten-second trip, we arrived at our destination. This island was more of an agriculture-based area. Crops that looked like wheat, barley, and corn sprouted up in fields along the roadways. There were warehouses to hold and process the crops and enclaves of small cottages where people seemed to live. There was no one working in the fields, only automated machines. The canal system was present, and I guessed that these canals would be fresh water to use on the crops, while the ones on the other islands were very likely salt water. Just a guess, and it didn't matter anyway. People were out on small boats on the canals, and I thought I saw some of them fishing. It was hard to tell how tall they were, but they all had hair. Some of the women had hair draping down their backs. A few of them glanced up at us, but no one seemed to mind us being there, which was a change. A change for the better, in my opinion.

It was the end of the road for us in terms of transit by tube since we had no money. Wait, let me clarify. We didn't think we had any money since we'd been rejected by the first tube on the last island. But there might have been a little money left on the wristbands. We simply didn't know how to check them. Gwen had the idea to follow one of the canals and see if there were boats we could access along the way, and sure enough, as we reached the edge of the island, there was a tiny marina of sorts where some of the boats were tied up. We approached one of the boats. Gwen held out her wristband toward the boat.

"Hold your wristband out," she said. "Maybe between us, we have enough money to rent one of these things."

I held out my wristband, and the panel blocking our access to the boat slid to the side. We got on board. It was likely a fusion-powered boat about fifteen feet long and relatively narrow. This boat was not meant to be driven in open water. The fact was that I had yet to see a vessel of any size on the open water. Only in the canals. There were four seats lined up in a row from front to back, the first seat directly behind the steering wheel. There was a start button to the left of the wheel and some kind of meter to the right. The meter displayed Arian numbers.

"Do you remember how the Arian number system works?" I asked.

"It's the same Hindu-Arabic system that is used on Earth. Positional base 10. That's why they used numbers like 100, 10 million, and one billion to describe their population to us. But they translated their numbers to ours so we could understand them. I don't know their symbols, but two digits are showing on that meter, meaning it's less than a hundred of something. Probably either the fuel amount or the amount of time we were able to rent the boat for. My guess is time, but I don't know anything about their time system either. Do you?"

"No, but my guess is it's probably not a lot of time since there's enough space on that meter for five digits, and we only have two."

"What do you think happens when time expires?" she asked.

"Maybe the boat just stops running," I said.

"Maybe," she said. "But it could be an honor system kind of thing. I mean, these people all seem very rule-oriented, right? So when the boat meter reaches zero, they pull it ashore and park it. Makes sense to me."

I wasn't so sure, but there was no doubt who was running our two-person show, so I went with it. "Where to?" I asked.

"Out there," she said, pointing at the vast expanse of ocean beyond the mouth of canal. "And let's toss these wristbands out here. They're no good to us anymore and they might be using them to track us."

We ripped the bands from our wrists and dropped them into the water.

Chapter 20

I don't think these boats are meant to go out in the ocean, Gwen," I said. "I think they're just for going on the canals. I haven't seen one boat in the ocean since we arrived, and I've been looking."

"The water looks very calm," she said. "And we know the planet has no moon, so the tides are also very tame."

"All true," I said. "But where do we go?"

"Let's put our 20/5 vision to use," she said. "It's like having built-in binoculars."

"What are we looking for?" I asked.

"Look for the dome; if you don't see that, look for an island with no tube connection from sky or water."

We both scanned the horizon. There was no sign of the dome, but at least three islands at the very edge of the horizon looked to be without tube service. I knew Gwen could see them too. "Which one do you prefer?" I asked.

"Let's take the one in the center," she said. "It's the biggest one."

"Sounds good," I said, but it really didn't sound good. It sounded like a disaster in the making.

I started the boat and steered it out of the canal and into the ocean. The water was smooth. Not as gentle as the water on Earth Station, but surprisingly calm. I wondered if the extra gravity helped hold the water in place better. I'm no physicist, but it made sense to me. There were still a few concerns, however, such as how long the boat would keep running and why there were no other boats out there. I watched the gauge, and it didn't move for a while, suggesting we might be okay in terms of having a working vehicle for the duration of our trip. We kept moving in the direction of the island we'd chosen. It didn't seem to be getting any bigger, which meant it was a long way away, and when I glanced back at the island we had come from, it was noticeably smaller than when we had started. The gauge ticked down a notch but was still double digits. I wasn't worried, much. But then Gwen shrieked.

"What the fuck is that?" she screamed.

I looked over to the left and saw a massive snake-like body under the water, passing by the boat. It was a grayish color and broader than a sperm whale. Its body kept going by for so long that it seemed as long as a football field.

"This is not good, Gwen. I think we figured out why there are no boats out here."

"Maybe we should turn around and head back," she said, panic in her voice.

"Good idea," I said, but I never got the chance to make the turn.

Directly in front of us, the creature reared up out of the water with opened jaws, laden with rows of curved fangs the size and shape of scimitars, poised to swallow the entire boat and us along with it. I veered off sharply just as it lunged at us. It missed us by inches and would surely be coming up for another attack soon.

"Do you think you can talk to that thing?" screamed Gwen, hysterical but remembering my unique ability nonetheless. Thank goodness she had because I was drawing a complete blank on finding a way out of this.

"No idea," I said, "but it's worth a try. Take the wheel, will you?"

The serpent rose up in front of our boat, ready to finish us, and I opened my mind to try and establish a link, and I felt it. It was like the moment you feel a fish grab the hook. Subtle, but you feel it. The link was rough, but it was there, so I sent a thought into its mind. You will remember that this kind of thought communication isn't about words at all. So when I try to communicate what was said, it only approximates what actually occurred. But words are what you understand, so words

I will give you. I can't remember exactly what my first thought message to the monster was, but it was something like, *We are friends and want to talk to you.*

The hideous beast stopped in its tracks but kept its head above the water, using the rest of its body to maneuver to the side of our boat. Its head was only about five feet from us, so close that we could smell its rotten breath, full of the foul odor of death. But I had its attention, so I needed to keep the momentum going.

We are humans from another world, I said. *We want to know all the living things here on this planet. In this ocean. You are the most magnificent creature we have ever seen.*

I mean, guys, I know. But what would you do or say in the same situation? If you had one chance to placate a three hundred-foot-long ocean cobra into not swallowing you and your boat whole? Anyway, it worked. The thing sent a thought back to me, and by the way, I felt a maleness in his presence, so I'm going to refer to him as such rather than call him "it."

My kind has roamed the oceans since the beginning. We are the Guardians of the Sea. By arrangement with the New Arians, we are to keep the oceans clear of their kind in exchange for them leaving us alone.

Well, that was news. I didn't know the difference between a New Arian and an Old Arian at that point, but I felt like we were getting somewhere, nonetheless. *We were not told of these rules. We will gladly return to the island we came from.*

The serpent seemed to be thinking about this.

Where are you going? What is your true purpose here?

Maybe he didn't buy my story about wanting to study his kind, but we were still alive. Perhaps honesty was now called for.

We are trying to find out the truth about what is happening here on this planet.

What truth do you seek?

We seek to find out if the humans in charge have secrets.

Oh yes, they have secrets, said the beast.

Now we were getting somewhere! *We seek to learn more on the island ahead.*

Are you carrying tracking wristbands?

What? Those things were to track us? I thought they were to dispense money. But it didn't matter because we no longer had them.

We threw them into the water back at the island we came from.

Very well, then. You may proceed. But make haste. You cannot be seen out here.

The serpent dove beneath the surface and disappeared, but I sensed he was nearby, not far below us. He was following us to ward off any other predators that might approach. Wow, I never thought my ability to communicate with other species would be *that* handy.

Gwen reached over and hugged me. "I love you, Wild Man," she said. And she never stopped calling me that the rest of the time we knew one another.

Chapter 21

It turned out that the honor system we'd hoped the Arians used for the boat rentals was a bad call because our little boat stopped running before we made it to the island. I sent a message to our friend below us, and he graciously offered to help. Within seconds, I felt our boat being nudged from below, and it rose out of the water. Thank goodness there was no keel, and it was nearly a flat-bottomed boat, designed for short transits along canals because a more streamlined shape would have resulted in us tipping over and falling overboard. But it worked. I looked down and saw our boat resting on the head of the serpent, and this made sense because he propelled himself by undulating the rest of his body, like a snake on land would. A side benefit was that the speed of our transit improved using this newly discovered method of travel, and within ten minutes, we were nearing the island.

The serpent told me he didn't want to frighten the people on shore by bringing us all the way there. Instead, he would speed up and give us a boost of momentum to help us coast the rest of the way. We accelerated somewhat dramatically, and then I felt the boat sink back into the water and race toward the shore. I looked back and saw the massive head of the serpent above the water, watching us. *You will find the truth there*, was his parting thought; then his monstrous head disappeared below the surface. I wondered if we would ever see him again. I hoped we would.

Unfortunately, we didn't quite make it to shore. The boat slowly coasted to a halt about a hundred feet from the gently breaking waves on the beach. There were people there, and I was surprised that several of them entered the water and began swimming toward us. I counted six of them. When they arrived at the boat, one yelled at me.

"Blee pal bate ta shore," he said.

It was Arian, but in a dialect so different from what we had learned, it was nearly a foreign language. All became clear, however, when they surrounded the boat and began pushing and pulling it toward the "shore," the one word I had recognized in his statement. It took a while, but we got there. Gwen and I jumped off and helped the men pull the boat as far up onto the sand as possible. They seemed content that it was far enough up on the beach not to be pulled back in by high tide because they began walking toward the forest up ahead. One of them smiled and waved for us to come with them. We followed.

The group leading us was composed of four men and two women. All of them were demonstratively shorter than the Arians, even shorter than us. Both genders were stocky and heavily muscled. The men wore loose swimsuits made of white, stretchy fabric and were bare-chested and hairy. The women wore identical suits as the men and a bandeau of the same material over their breasts. The women had fine hair on their legs and under their arms but none on their faces, whereas the men had full beards. These people were indeed quite hairy, but it was refreshing at least that their private parts weren't on display for the world to see, as ours were since we were wearing the Arian garb. I made a mental note to ask for some of those clothes at the appropriate moment.

They took us into the forest, and I heard the faint sounds of music. We walked along a path made of smooth stone and soon emerged in a public square surrounded entirely by the forest. By the way, this wasn't a tropical island. Aria had a mild climate, similar to the weather in the White Mountains during summer. So there were no palm trees here. Instead, the trees were deciduous and resembled beech trees. Smooth bark and oval-shaped leaves with toothed edges.

The area we went to was like a walking mall, full of small shops and food vendors. The source of the music was a band of three people playing instruments that vaguely resembled a harp, a flute, and a banjo. They played a tune that sounded something like Irish music, and when the man with the banjo began to sing, even more so. And then I saw the children. Scurrying about and squealing the way children do when they're happy. It was all so pleasant, yet terribly disorienting because it existed in such stark contrast to what we had just come from. My confusion was soothed, however, when I caught sight of patrons drinking from mugs that looked like they held beer.

One of the women pointed to an empty table and encouraged us to sit down. The chairs were made of wood but beautifully carved, smooth, and comfortable. After we all sat, drinks were brought to our table, containing the ale I had mentioned. One of the men raised his mug and said. "Walecame!"

We hoisted our mugs and drank. Oh my, this was like a high-alcohol-content IPA. Powerful and delicious. So far, so good as far as I was concerned. Gwen didn't seem happy with the ale but sipped on it nonetheless. *I'm fine,* she thought. *Ecstatic, actually. This is so cool, Wild Man.* She smiled, and I felt even better.

"Wait isline ya came frim?" asked one of the men.

You will remember that Gwen and I had been given the ability to quickly assimilate languages, and it was already becoming easier to understand what was being said, so I'll save you the work and just write the conversation without burdening you with their accent from this point forward.

"We are not from an island," I said.

"Where, then?"

"We are from another planet."

"Oh, which one?"

"Earth."

"Never heard of it."

"What is the name of this island?" I asked.

"True Eden," said the man.

I was confused, and even more so when I saw the group of people at our table smiling.

"This place is the true birthplace of humanity," said the man. "First Eden is a sham."

Chapter 22

And so the truth of Aria unfolded in front of us, told by the man who seemed to be a leader of some sort, whose name was Mada. Eons ago, there had been a great war. Those who wanted to advance against those who were happy as they were. Not unlike struggles that have occurred throughout the ages on Earth. On Aria, it was what Mada called the "New Arians" against his kind, the "True Arians." The New against the True, as he put it. And, of course, the True never stood a chance. At that point in history, the technology of the New Arians was highly advanced, and they easily defeated the True Arians, relegating them to islands like this one and essentially imprisoning them by preventing them from leaving. No tubes, no boats, no planes. And just to make sure, a deal was struck with the Guardians to keep all humans off the water.

The Guardians had fought alongside the True but had been no match for the weapons of the New Arians. They quickly abandoned the cause, making a truce with New Aria that had held to this day, with a few exceptions. The result would have been a reasonably happy ending for everyone except for one thing. The True Arians and the Guardians knew the truth about the New Arians. The way they entertained themselves and enhanced themselves.

I promise to tell you, and I will, but it was a lot to take in. One step at a time. First, let's talk more about the True. How they lived. What was important to them. True Eden was a large island, about the size of Cuba, where over eleven million people lived when I was on Earth. I never found out how many people lived on True Eden, but it wasn't eleven million, probably not even a million. The True were more primitive, technologically, than the New Arians, but they weren't stupid. They understood they had limited resources and took steps to make them last. They recycled everything, limited the number of children a couple could bear, and never wasted anything.

I learned that the True had made their own arrangement with the Guardians, a side deal of sorts. How did they do this? Turns out the True could communicate with animals, just like me. I can't explain to you how that made me feel, but it somehow bonded me to them and them to me. I was immediately granted acceptance into their culture. Gwen was treated nicely, don't get me wrong, but something was happening on a deeper level between me and the True, and I think it had to do with the talking with animals thing. Gwen could see the bond, and she was glad for it. I'm sure she would have been fine there without me but I suppose it was reassuring to her that I was tight with the natives.

Anyway, back to the agreement between the True and the Guardians. The True weren't allowed to take boats out on the water, but the Guardians let them swim in the shallow waters to hunt and protected them from other predators while they were out there. Trust me when I tell you that some of the other predators were far more treacherous than any sea creature that lived on Earth. I know because I had an encounter with one I'll tell you about soon. But the Guardians were still the top dog in the oceans of Aria, and they insured the safety of the True while they were out in the water. The True used spearguns to hunt fish and nets to catch the sea life that swam in schools, like shrimp. Of course, none of the species found in the seas of Aria were duplicates of what was found on Earth, or vice versa, but it's just easier if I call the fish "fish" and the shrimp "shrimp" and the crabs, "crab." They were all there, and if they didn't look exactly like their distant cousins on Earth, they certainly tasted like them.

The True lived in houses built from wood, but they had no fusion power or electricity. They didn't want it, having seen what it did to those who had embraced "advancement." You may wonder how the True felt about the New Arians, and the answer goes a long way to describing who these people really were. You see, they pitied them. Didn't hate them for imprisoning them. If anything, they were grateful for being allowed to live how they wanted to live. For me, it was difficult to filter out the anger I felt toward the New Arians, especially after I learned why they had been seeding other planets with humanity for the past fifty thousand years.

There were actually two reasons. The first was pure entertainment. The New Arians always deployed drones on the planets they colonized, and among other things, these drones had cameras that could film what was going on and beam it back to the New Arians. As the number of new worlds expanded, so did the entertainment options for the humans on New Aria, and that's what they were doing behind the closed doors that we never got to walk through in their capital city.

When the Makers allowed them to travel the Pathways of the universe, the New Arians could access these worlds whenever they wanted, planting more drone cameras so the entertainment could continue as the civilizations advanced. They could watch anything they wanted. Wars, murders, rapes, but also beautiful things, like babies being born, animals living freely in the wild, and people in love, sharing intimacies behind closed doors. They used this entertainment to enhance their pathetic lives, filling them with feelings and desires they could no longer foster on their own. And they would have fallen prey to what the Teacher had explained before our trip, the lethargy that affects advanced societies, except they didn't stop at simply watching video feeds from the colonial worlds.

The New Arians developed a system to prevent this supposedly inevitable despondency from happening. The Human Purity scale. The True knew what it was, and while they didn't practice it, nor were they even included in the annual Purity Census, they were aware of the details and described them to us. We knew there were five categories but didn't know what they were until we met the True.

Category One was Physical Beauty, the parameters of which had produced the people we saw in First Eden, a city of ten million clones, all built based on someone's preconceived notion of what Physical Beauty should be. Someone who had looked exactly like them, no doubt. The first "One," it was assumed. By then, the True had already been segregated from the New Arians, so they didn't know for sure. It seemed logical that someone in power had decided what Physical Beauty was and defined it to be themselves. It didn't matter. It happened.

Category Two was Voice Command. The ability to motivate others using the tone and modulation of your voice. I remembered the words we were asked to recite:

You will obey. It goes without saying that Gwen scored a lot higher than I did on that one.

Category Three was Raw Intelligence. Category Four was Ambition, closely related to Category Five, Ingenuity. Three, Four, and Five were the ones where the AI somehow went into our brains and established a score for each area. I remember Gwen telling me she obtained a 19 in Category Four, which we now understood to be Ambition, and I wasn't surprised. Nor was I surprised by her score of 18 in Ingenuity. She was a "very clever girl" in every sense of the word clever. But there was more relevance to Categories Four and Five than Gwen's score in each area.

Ambition and Ingenuity were the missing links in the New Arians' formula for self-preservation. Just as Homo Erectus was the missing link in human evolution, Ambition and Ingenuity were the missing links in human survival over time. When a civilization loses Ambition because it has delegated all tasks to AI and machines, it loses its humanity. Not only the urge to learn more—Ambition—but the means to do it—Ingenuity. As ambition declined, so did ingenuity. It seemed you needed to use these traits for them to be retained by the species. Ambition and Ingenuity could wane over one lifetime and from generation to generation unless stimulated to maintain themselves. In a society where there were no natural challenges, it was difficult to sustain these two attributes.

I asked Mada why the New Arians hadn't lost their Ambition and Ingenuity, and the second reason for them seeding planets with humanity was revealed. These human traits could be renewed if you knew where to look.

"They go to the Zoo," he said.

Chapter 23

The domes covered the Zoos. According to Mada, there were two kinds of zoos on Aria. The first kind was where the Homo Erectus were trained before they were dispatched to whatever distant world they'd been assigned to. Apparently, they were placed into an environment that simulated the one where they would be going to "acclimate" them to the conditions there. Unfortunately, for some, this meant death before they ever left Aria, but the ones who survived were well-prepared to thrive in their new homes. The evidence of that was plentiful here on Aria and was housed in the second kind of zoo.

The other kind of zoo contained humans from off-world. Mada explained that the first three categories on the Human Purity scale could be obtained with little trouble if you had enough money. The perfectly engineered body could be made. The more money you had, the better body you could buy. The voice could be artificially enhanced and honed to perfection through practice. Raw Intelligence could also be introduced during the reengineering process through AI infusion. But Ambition and Ingenuity could not be artificially produced.

Therefore, humans from the colonies with high Ambition and/or Ingenuity scores were brought to the zoos on Aria and stored for when needed. Whenever subjects were identified with an Ingenuity score of 15 or above, they were selected for deportation from their home world to Aria and eventually removed by the AI-operated drones stationed on every planet. I speculated that these could be the UFOs reported on from time to time on Earth. But that didn't matter.

"What are the living conditions like in these zoos?" I asked.

"We don't know," said Mada. "We have never been close to those islands."

"But how do you know what they are?" asked Gwen.

"The Guardians," said Mada. "They communicate with some of the residents."

"Wouldn't that be enough for the Guardians to determine the living conditions?" asked Gwen.

"I suppose it would," he said. "If the question was asked. But why would a Guardian, who lives in a hostile world under the sea, even think to ask such a question?"

Mada explained that the Guardians were the most intelligent beings on the planet. Their brains were by far the largest, and while they had gigantic bodies, they didn't need giant brains to make those bodies work. I remembered something I read about the great Brontosaurus having a brain the size of a tennis ball. But not the Guardians. The descriptions from the True led me to visualize brains as big as a baby elephant. The Guardians' flaw, of course, was that they had no appendages. No hands or fingers to manipulate matter, as humans did. All they had were their massive jaws and deadly fangs.

"It must be frustrating for them to think so clearly yet accomplish so little," I said.

"They accomplish more than you might think," said Mada. "They keep the peace on this planet."

"But they have no choice in the matter," said Gwen. "It's that or be destroyed by the New Arians."

"There is always a choice," said Mada. "My people have chosen to live our lives in peace and harmony. We are happy to let the New Arians decide their own fate as long as they leave us alone."

"But there's no guarantee of that," said Gwen. "In time, they may find uses for you just as they've found uses for humans from other planets."

"Perhaps," said Mada. "But that time has not yet come."

"We need to learn more about these zoos," I said.

"How?" he asked.

"Do you think one of the Guardians would take me to one of them?" I asked.

"I doubt that very much," he said.

"If we gave them the questions to ask of the people there, would they be willing to ask them?" asked Gwen.

"That I believe they would do."

*****

Gwen and I agreed on a list of questions and then walked down to the beach, accompanied by Mada. I didn't send out any signals trying to call one of the serpents, but before long, I saw the wake of one heading our way, and it didn't stop. The head emerged and kept on coming, right up onto the beach and to within five feet of where we were standing. The thing's mouth wasn't open, so I wasn't afraid it would eat us or anything like that. I just wasn't sure what to do next, but then Mada cleared things up.

"The serpent has agreed to go to the nearest Zoo and get answers to your questions. You may convey them to him now."

I linked with the big guy's mind and could immediately tell that it was the same one that had nearly killed us. I would learn from the Mada that there were six

Guardians patrolling the coasts of this island to prevent boating, and all of them were in on the ruse to allow the True to fish the shallow waters. Anyway, I gave this one the information we were trying to obtain; he rose up and turned back to the sea, slithering away and leaving tracks in the sand wider than a Mack truck.

We went back to the open area and had some food and beer. One of the women came over to Gwen and brought her a clear container that vaguely resembled a wine glass, filled with a liquid that looked like white wine, and I thought Gwen might pass out with joy. She sipped it, and if you could have seen the smile on her face, you would have been as buoyant as I was.

"I wonder how they knew you liked white wine," I said.

"They're mind readers," she said.

"How do you know?"

"Takes one to know one," she said, taking a long pull from her glass of wine. "I'm surprised you didn't pick that up."

"Other things on my mind, I guess." Like what the heck we were doing here and how we would survive this so I could get back my dogs and One-eyed Jack.

Mada told us they had prepared a place nearby for us to stay and was about to take us there when I saw him tilt his chin in the air as if he'd heard something important.

"We need to return to the beach," he said. "The Guardian is there."

"How could he be back so soon?" I asked. "It's only been a few hours."

"The Guardians are the fastest swimmers in the sea. Faster than anything on Aria, except the tube cylinders."

When we got back to the shore, the serpent was already on the beach, and I suspect he could have come all the way to the center of town if he'd wanted to. Later, I learned that the Guardians could go on land but had agreed not to as part of their truce with the New Arians that ended the ancient war. But that's another story. Right now, you need to know what he had to say.

I assumed that Mada was receiving the same information I was because as I watched his face, it contorted in expressions of fear, anger, and remorse. I'm sure mine did as well. The Guardian had learned that all the humans came to the Zoos from the Skytubes. All were off-worlders. There was a new batch every Rev. During the course of a Rev, the prisoners were processed in some kind of facility and then sent to the Skytube and taken away. No one was killed. The ones that resisted were stunned and dragged into the processing facility, then taken away to the tube after being processed.

What goes on in there? I asked. *In the processing facilities.*

No one knows for sure, but they think something is removed from the person's mind and not returned, said the Guardian.

How do they know this?

Because the people are not the same when they come out as when they went in. More docile. More compliant.

That could be drugs, I suggested.

Perhaps, said the Guardian, then he turned away and disappeared into the water.

When I conveyed the information to Gwen, she figured it out immediately.

"They're harvesting the Ambition and Ingenuity from these people. And then they sell them to the highest bidder."

"You think they can harvest only a piece of someone's Essence? I asked. "I don't think even the Makers can do that."

"That's what I think," she said. "And you know what else I think?"

"What?"

"I need to get Maddie and bring her here. She has the power to deal with this, and I believe in my heart she'll want to help."

Chapter 24

Absolutely," I said. "When do we leave?"

She reached out and took my hand. "You need to stay here, Zach."

"Why?"

"Think about all the Arian laws we've broken already. It's going to take a tall tale to talk them into letting us off the planet, and that's my specialty, having spent most of my adult life in politics. You, on the other hand, well, let's just say it's not your thing."

"How can you say that?" I asked. "I mean, I write novels, for Christ's sake. I make things up for a living."

"Writing is one thing," she said. "Acting is another. You wear your emotions on your sleeve, Zach. It's one of the things I love about you. I always know where I stand with you. But that's not what's called for here, and you know it."

I was getting agitated, or more to the point, scared. Scared for her.

"How do you plan on getting home?" I asked.

Gwen described her scheme to us, and it was a wild one. I struggled to believe she could even pull off phase one. She asked Mada and me to talk one of the Guardians into taking her all the way back to First Eden and, not only that, for the Guardian to tell the lie that would get her onto land. After that, she said she would improvise based on the situation. I was well aware that she was good at improvising. After all, she'd received an 18 out of 20 on Ingenuity, compared to my score of 12, but the lack of clarity was worrisome to me.

Nevertheless, we had to do something, not only to save the helpless victims in the domes but to save ourselves. And while I'm ashamed to admit it, I knew that if we were going to be saved, it would be Gwen and, hopefully, Maddie that got the job done. I'm not a coward, don't misunderstand me here. I'm just not as resourceful as those two. It also made sense that one of us remained behind in the event her plan failed. To try another approach. I had no idea what that might be, and I didn't want to think about it because that meant believing that Gwen would be unsuccessful, either dying on the way to First Eden or being imprisoned upon her arrival there.

We summoned a Guardian, and the same one as the previous times appeared. This side of the island was his assigned area, so it would always be him if we came to this side. The best translation of his name, by the way, was Alfred, believe it or not, which means "wise counselor."

I asked him if we could call him "Al," and he didn't object, so that's what I'll call him here. We reviewed the plan with him, and he agreed to help us. I got the impression that he wasn't at all worried about himself or his kind, but he did point out that Gwen would be in trouble when he dropped her off at First Eden, having broken so many laws of the New Arians. Stealing, boating on the open sea, contact with uncivilized humans, and even corruption of a Guardian were on the list. But it didn't matter. She'd made up her mind, telling me her gut was pushing her to do this, which always worked out. It was useless to resist her.

I wish I could tell you that we went to the guest home provided by Mada and made passionate love before she left, but frankly, neither of us was in the mood. We were anxious and scared, and amorous feelings were far down the list of emotions we were experienced at that pivotal moment. We shared a meal together at the open area of the True, eating in silence, and then I accompanied her to the beach. But it wasn't just me. The entire village came with us. While we were waiting for Al to arrive, several men kneeled in front of Gwen and bowed their heads, some sign of respect and good wishes. The women lined up to kiss her on the cheek. It was as if the combined will of the True was being summoned to help her get through this.

Al slithered magnificently up onto the beach and lowered his head onto the sand. A group of True brought a wooden ladder from the forest and placed it on the side of Al's head, and Gwen and I approached it together. She turned to me, and I saw fear in her eyes, but not doubt. She was going to do this.

"I'll come back for you, Wild Man," she said, lurching forward and embracing me tightly.

"If you don't, I'm coming after you," I said, fighting off tears.

"Okay," she said and gave me a melancholy smile.

She let go of me and approached the ladder, ascending carefully. When she reached the top, I noticed that Al had somehow grown handles of some sort for Gwen to hold onto. He told me at a later time that they were antennae that the Guardians used to communicate with one another. They could send messages to each other from anywhere in the world using these antennae, another extraordinary power of theirs that further amazed me because it had developed naturally, over the eons, and wasn't gifted to them by superior beings like our enhanced abilities had been.

When Gwen was on top of Al's head and holding onto one of his antennae with one hand, she raised the other, waved to the crowd, then gave a short speech. I mean, that was Gwen. Always on stage.

"There's one thing the New Arians missed when they developed their Human Purity scale," she said, her voice clear, loud, and persuasive. "Humans will always yearn for something the Arians have not accounted for. And that is freedom. Freedom to choose our own destinies. I know you think you're free here, but that's not true. You understand in your hearts that you would do more if given the chance to do so. But that doesn't matter. What matters is that the system here is broken. Humans should not be processed for spare parts. And their human ancestors, the Homo Erectus, should not be bred so that more human slaves can be captured and used tens of thousands of years later. The New Arians have built an artificial society on the backs of real humans. True Humans. I promise you, one way or another, we will bring freedom back to the people of Aria!"

A cheer erupted from the True but not from me. I watched Gwen, in awe of her courage and frightened by her recklessness. On the other hand, I was happy for her because she was back in the game she had missed so terribly after vacating the office of the President. She was doing something important to her and others, and she obviously loved it, even though it might mean an abrupt ending to her life. I didn't want to think about that. Suddenly, her fiery eyes locked on mine. *I'm not leaving you, Wild Man. Our time together is only just beginning.*

I'll hold you to that, Gwen. Be safe.

Al raised his tremendous head and turned toward the water, winding through the sand and leaving a wide ditch in his wake. He swam out to sea and was picking up speed rapidly. Gwen was holding on with two hands, no doubt scared shitless, as I would have been had I been in her shoes. She turned her head and nodded, and I'm sure she would have waved if she hadn't needed to be holding on for dear life. After a few moments, they disappeared from sight, and I turned back to the True, tears streaming down my face.

Chapter 25

One

I received a message from a Guardian that he was bringing a human to me that he'd found in the ocean. She'd been with a man, who the Guardian had killed. But his reading of the woman indicated she might be of some value to me, so he was returning her to First Eden.

I sent One Hundred to fetch her and to bring her to me. I didn't worry that Gwendolyn Marks would try to escape. After her ordeal with the Guardian, she would undoubtedly be grateful to be alive and prostrate herself in front of me to beg for my temperance in rendering judgment upon her. She had broken many laws, and that would need to be addressed. But what interested me more was her true motivation. Why had she done it? Why had she gone out into the ocean in the first place? I would soon find out.

One Hundred took her to cleanse before bringing her to me. She seemed no worse for wear when she arrived at my apartment, dressed in my people's colorful, translucent garb. I must admit that something about her was attractive, although I couldn't quite figure out what it was. She was shapely, albeit short, and with hair, but shapeliness was the norm for women here in First Eden, and hair was distasteful. No, it was something else entirely that drew me to her. Something about her aura. A power emanated from her that couldn't be categorized by our system. What was it? Why couldn't I understand it?

"Welcome back, Gwendolyn," I said in my most gracious voice.

"Thank you for seeing me," she said, bowing her head slightly but not falling to her knees as I had hoped. "I want to explain all that has happened and seek your permission to return to my people."

Her voice command was good. Very good because I was already softening, actually considering her preposterous request. This would not do. "Leave us please, One Hundred."

One Hundred left the room, and the Earthling and I were alone. I adjusted my frame of mind so that her voice could not impact my feelings. She was mine to do with as I pleased, and I was considering doing just that, regardless of the implications for her well-being. After all, she was a criminal. There were no courts necessary here on Aria. Our system rendered One as the final arbitrator on all criminal and political matters; for this Rev, that responsibility was mine.

"Three tubes away, at the bottom of a canal, is where we found your wristbands," I said. "A pleasure boat was missing and still hasn't been recovered. Where is it?"

"It ran out of fuel, and then the monster came," she said, a flash of horror passing over her face, remembrances of her encounter with the Guardian.

"Are you saying he destroyed the boat?" I asked.

"That is my memory," she said. "Among other things." She cast her eyes down.

"I'm sorry your friend was lost," I said, compassion in my voice. Perhaps my sympathy would wring the truth from her.

"It was terrible," she said, beginning to break down.

"Now, now, Gwendolyn. You are safe and lucky to be so. The Guardians are wise creatures, however, and this one realized that you were…special."

"How so?" she asked.

"You have qualities that are valued here on Aria. Please, come sit with me. We can talk."

I walked over to the meeting place and took my seat. She sat down across from me.

"What will happen to me?" she asked.

"That depends," I said.

"On what?"

"On you telling me the truth about why you ventured out three tube stops and then stole a boat to go… where?"

"We were just having fun, enjoying ourselves! No one told us there was a law against boating on the ocean."

"Just a pleasure cruise then? Is that it?"

"Yes."

The woman was obviously lying. I sent a message to the AI to read her mind and was surprised when it came back to me with nothing of importance, claiming she had a mind block in a section of her brain that held her secrets. My frustration was mounting.

"Gwendolyn, the truth will come out, one way or another. It would be easier for you to tell me now."

"I've told you the truth, One, and I want to leave now. The Makers will not be happy to hear that one of our group has been killed and the other is being held captive here."

"Let me clarify things for you then. First, the Makers will be informed that both you and your pathetic partner were killed after being explicitly warned not to venture out into the open water."

"Are you going to kill me, then?"

"Of course not. You will be taken somewhere where you can be of use to us. The truth will also come out when you are there."

"Where is that?" she asked.

"You are going to the Zoo," I informed her.

I instructed the AI to stun her and transfer the body to the nearest Zoo for processing. I also put in my bid to purchase her Ambition and Ingenuity for future use, and I made the price so high that her exceptional qualities would be mine and only mine when I needed them. No one else would have the opportunity to equal my scores in these categories. Not as long as I was One.

Chapter 26

Word came to us from the Guardian that Gwen had been safely delivered to First Eden. I stayed in Mada's village for a long time after that. Too long. It was still daylight, but the skies were beginning to darken slightly, so I knew many days had passed. Mada was the village leader, an enclave of about a thousand people who lived off the fish of the sea and fruit from the trees. Each family had their own vegetable garden and grew things similar to tomatoes and cucumbers. I lived in the tiny house they had loaned me, initially intended for Gwen and me to share. I missed her terribly, and the more time that passed, the more somber my mood became.

Mada had a wife and two children, a boy who looked to be eleven or twelve and a girl of around eight years of age. His wife's name was Lalia, and she helped to take care of me, bringing me food and comforting me with stories of life on True Eden when I was gloomy, more frequent as time passed.

Mada had an unmarried sister named Nadia, who also befriended me and visited me often. She was a beautiful young woman, and it didn't take long for me to figure out that she wanted more from me than friendship. One day she showed up with a basket of food, and I noticed she had shaved her legs and under her arms and smelled of fresh soap. She wore shorter and tighter shorts than the women typically wore, and the wrapping around her breasts was more revealing. It was hard to understand how an alluring woman in her twenties could be attracted to a man in his early fifties, especially a man without a penny to his name and so melancholy to boot. Still, her affection for me was confirmed by Mada one day while we drank ale in the open square.

"My sister likes you," he said. "Why do you reject her?"

Surprised, I was at a loss for words. "I don't understand," I said.

"She is a single woman, and you are a single man. Coming together is the way of things when both parties are willing."

"But I'm not single, Mada. I'm with Gwen."

A shadow passed over Mada's face when I said that. It wasn't anger about my resistance to his sister. It was something about Gwen. "What is it?" I asked him. "What are you trying to tell me, Mada?"

"It's not likely she will return," he said, bowing his head.

I felt anger pass through me when he said this, followed by a tremor of fear. "Why? Why won't she return?"

"The New Arians are heartless people," he said. "They will use her for whatever purpose suits them. But they will not release her."

"Why didn't you express this opinion before she left?" I asked.

"It is not our way to interfere with the path others take," was his answer. Translation: *We are grateful to be left alone and grant the same respect to others.*

Despair overwhelmed me. I drank more and more beer, trying and failing to get drunk due to my advanced metabolism, but Mada had more news for me.

"You and I must travel tomorrow," he said.

I raised my head up, shaking off the cobwebs of despair. "Where?"

"We must go to a special meeting of the Council of True Eden."

"Why? Why do I need to go? I should be here, waiting for Gwen."

"The meeting is about you," he said.

"What? Why does the Council care about me?"

"You are an outsider," he said. "The first to come here in many generations. Some fear this will bring retribution from New Aria."

"But no one knows I'm here. If they did, they would have already come for me."

"The Guardians know you are here," said Mada. "Some do not trust the Guardians because they made a deal with the New Arians long ago that caused us to be confined here. Some believe the Guardians will reveal your presence here if something is to be gained for it."

"I don't believe that!" I said. "The Guardians have helped us. They help you. Every fish you catch, every swarm of shrimp you net, comes from the goodwill of the Guardians. They gain nothing from allowing you to do this and risk their own well-being."

Mada smiled, reaching out to touch me on the arm. "I understand what you say, my friend Zach, and I agree. Come with me to the Council meeting, and together we will convince them."

*****

We left the next day on foot, traveling through the deep forest that seemed to go on forever. I had forsaken my shoes since they filled with sand even during a short walk, and my feet had grown used to being bare. The paths were soft, laden with a mix of sand and dirt, and the foot was a fantastic appendage. Far more adaptable than many other parts of the body that get more attention.

Darkness had come now and would be with us for fifteen Earth Days, but neither Mada nor I suffered because both of us saw well at night. And when I say it was night, I mean it was terribly dark. There is no moon circling Aria that might reflect the light of the sun to help show the way, only stars of a part of the Milky Way that was 580 light years from Earth. I recognized none of them, but the subtle light they shone upon the land was enough for us to find our way.

We walked for what seemed like a full Earth day, and eventually, the forest began to thin, giving way to fields of crops and then to homes and roads that led to a city of some sort. People working in the fields stood up and stared at us, and I assumed they were looking at me, half a head taller than Mada and much more narrowly configured. The further we went, the more tightly packed the buildings became, but none of them were made from the silvery material found on the islands of New Aria that Gwen and I had passed through on our way to this magical place. The homes were made of wood, and the roofs were some thinly shaved rocks, like slate, but much lighter in color, perhaps from the presence of sand in their composition. There were windows of glass, which didn't surprise me since sand was an abundant resource here and the primary raw material for glass.

We entered the city, walking now on streets of flat stones grouped together like cobblestones and secured by some kind of cement. Shops, restaurants, and bars lined the streets, and people were everywhere, gawking as we passed by, wondering where the obvious outsider had come from, no doubt. We turned right on a wide avenue, and up ahead, I saw a large round building that looked like a small stadium.

"That is where the Council meets," said Mada, pointing at the building. "Listen to me carefully from this point forward."

*****

I won't make you suffer through the details of the meeting of the Council, as I did. Suffice it to say that arguments were made for and against my presence on the island, and in the end, I was ordered to leave. I was allowed to speak and failed miserably at convincing enough of the village leaders to allow me to stay. If Gwen had been there to speak, I'm absolutely certain she would have turned some minds in our direction. But she wasn't there, and that only added to my sense of defeat and loneliness. The final vote was 53 for leaving and 47 for staying. One hundred villages, but not enough wanted to risk keeping me there.

When I asked how I would fulfill their wishes, I was told to leave the same way I arrived. The little boat that had been hidden in the trees after we towed it to shore. The boat with no power. What option did that leave me? Swimming? But then a wristband with money on it was produced, which would allow me to buy more power from the boat, and a new mystery unfolded. Where did they get the wristband? Mada explained that certain members of the Council maintained loose and unofficial contact with the New Arians and that news further soiled my perception of these people. Yes, nearly half of them had supported me, but what about the other half? Were they in the pocket of the New Arians? Not to be trusted, no matter how many smiles they gave me? Definitely not to be trusted.

"I'll get Al to help me," I said, confident that he would.

"I've already contacted him," said Mada. "He cannot be seen helping you now that the lie has been told that you are dead. But he will try to guard you from harm until you reach the shore of the nearest island."

"You mean, like following along under the water?" I asked.

"Yes, he will do his best, but there are no guarantees in the seas of Aria," said Mada.

"Well, it's better than nothing, I guess."

Mada was terribly embarrassed by the result of the Council vote, but he accepted it, promising to escort me back to his village and oversee my deportation. The entire thing seemed like a farce to me. Were they really going to force me to drive that little boat out into the vast ocean at night, my only hope being that Al would somehow protect me from harm? The harsh reality is that for Al, my death would probably close a can of worms that he didn't want open. He had no true incentive to help me to survive, especially knowing that I would be helpless to escape the planet even if I made it all the way back to First Eden.

We got back to the village, where I had been granted a stay of a few hours to gather supplies for my journey, but I wasn't inclined to gather supplies. I made my way to the beach.

I was surprised and moved when what seemed like the entire village accompanied me on my walk down the plank. I didn't have to touch the boat since a host of strong men dragged it to the water for me and held it there in the shallows, bobbing and waiting for me. I had a vision of myself swinging from a noose, bobbing and waiting like the boat, dangling there until someone cut me down and buried me. I looked into the crowd and saw Mada's wife and sister together. Both were crying, seeming to understand that I was facing a death sentence, about to be executed.

Mada approached me and embraced me tightly, and I didn't resist. Squeezed back a little even. "I am sorry, my friend. I tried."

"I'll be okay, Mada," I lied, then turned to leave.

"Wait!" he said, reaching into his pocket for something. I turned back to look at him. He withdrew a capsule that looked like a small test tube. It was filled with a clear liquid and had a cap on the top. He reached out with it, offering it to me.

"What is it?" I asked.

"It's hair-cleansing solution. Drink it, and all your hair will fall away. This could be of great help to you in disguising yourself, should you need it."

"Thank you," I said, taking the tube in my hand and placing it in my pocket. "How long does it take for it to work?"

"Minutes," he said.

"Then I'll take it only if I need it. No need to go to my grave as a bald man. Thank you, Mada."

He smiled grimly. "There is always hope, Zach."

I suppose that was true, but it was hard to feel any hope at that moment. I turned away from him again, walked down to the beach, waded into the water, and went to the boat, the vessel of my pending demise. I was lifted into the boat by the villagers. I held the wristband in front of the power meter, and it came to life. Five full digits appeared on the screen. Lots of money on that wristband. Perhaps I would have enough power to make it all the way to the First Eden. Ironic, really, leaving True Eden and heading to First Eden. Going in confusing directions on a world far away from my home. And while I expected not to make it far, I would try my best to drive the little boat all the way to the capital. And if by some miracle I made it, I would confront the man known as One and demand that he tell me what had happened to Gwen. I'd make up some lie that he might believe, and he would have no choice but to comply with my wishes. Yes, my wishes. Wishful thinking, no doubt.

The boat puttered out into the black waters. It was a cloudy night, so the sky and sea were as dark as dark could be. I could make out very little in front of me. Perhaps I wouldn't even see Al coming when he rose up to swallow me, fulfilling the Guardians' agreement with the New Arians. And if not him or one of his kind, some other monster from the depths would handle it. I glanced back and saw nothing. The island where humanity had been born was gone from my sight. Adding insult to injury, it began to rain. Slow and steady at first, but then a downpour. The seas boiled up in front of me, and I wondered if my fate would be to drown rather than be eaten. It didn't matter. I pushed the little boat forward into the dark and dangerous waters, resolved to go down fighting no matter what the universe threw at me.

PART THREE

Chapter 27

I imagine there are creatures of the night on every inhabited world in the universe, and Aria was no exception. Unfortunately, I found that out the hard way. I had survived the storm and continued to plow forward into the night, the waves still undulating, but at least the flood from the heavens had stopped. Luckily, the boat had some kind of automatic bailing system because there was no water sloshing around anymore, as had been the case during the storm. I saw lights in the distance and wondered if it was the island where we had stolen the boat or another one. It didn't matter because I was going there no matter what it was. I had that wristband full of money, at least. I figured it still had more money since it had filled the power tank of this boat with no trouble and undoubtedly had a reserve. I could spend it on the tubes to make my way back to First Eden. Things seemed to be turning in my favor, but then the boat started acting up.

The first sign of trouble was the stuttering of the propeller. I didn't know if that was due to engine problems, which seemed unlikely considering the invincibility of fusion technology, but then the boat fell dead in the water, yet I continued to hear the subtle whining of the drive shaft. Had the propeller fallen off? No idea. And things didn't stop there. I felt water on my bare feet and realized the boat was sinking. And as I looked closer, I could see that the floor of the boat was dissolving before my very eyes. I jumped onto one of the seats, but it soon began to rock, losing its connection with the rapidly disappearing floor. The boat was going down, but as I looked to dive overboard, I saw the outlines of a circular shape surrounding it. A mouth. An enormous mouth. Even broader than Al's mouth and about to take in the entire boat and myself. And where the heck was Al, anyway? Wasn't he supposed to be down there somewhere protecting me?

Refusing to give up, I leaped to the boat's bow, stood on its edge, bent my legs, and pushed off with all my might. I surprised myself because I easily cleared the mouth surrounding the boat and plunged into the water at least twenty feet away. Thank goodness for that extra strength. The boat disappeared, and so did the mouth that had swallowed it. I realized I was a dead man but nevertheless began stroking madly in a direction away from where the boat had gone down. I can't say I'm a fast swimmer, but I was making good time from sheer effort alone. To no avail. I felt a current underneath me and was slowly sucked under the water. There was nothing I could do to stop it, but I flailed on, taking one last breath before I was pulled under by whatever unthinkable monster was about to consume me.

Suddenly, I felt a distinct surge below me. It had a sound as well. Like the sound of a football tackle underwater. And then I was released, floating aimlessly on the surface of the dark water, suddenly alone. But not for long. A massive head emerged beside me, and I immediately recognized it was Al. He lowered his head and urged me to grab his antennae and pull myself up. I followed his instructions, flopping onto his gargantuan head like a fish flailing on the bottom of a boat after being reeled in. I can't tell you what relief I experienced. It was like sitting in the electric chair at 11:59 p.m. with the sentence to be carried out at midnight, only to have the governor grant a stay of execution, preserving my life for at least another day. After I caught my breath, we talked.

What the fuck was that thing? I asked.

A species called Flux that lives primarily in deep water, where light cannot penetrate. But they come to the surface for hunting when the long night arrives.

How did it disable the boat?

It dissolved the boat with a naturally-produced acid. It typically sprays the acid on the living tissues of its prey, but since you were protected by the boat, it had to take care of that first. You might also find it interesting that the acid begins the work of digestion before the beast ingests its prey.

Yeah, very interesting, Al. By the way, thank you for saving me. You are the nicest sea serpent I've ever met.

I don't know if Al had a sense of humor or if he could even laugh, but I sensed he got the joke. After all, he was supposedly among the most intelligent beings on this planet, which was saying something.

After I settled down, Al set off in what seemed to be a southerly direction, although I had long since lost my bearings and was just guessing.

Where are we going, Al? I asked.

To a remote Skytube station far from First Eden.

Why?

You must leave this planet and return with warriors.

Hmmm. *This doesn't sound good, Al. What's going on?*

Your friend, Gwendolyn, has been sent to a Zoo for processing. You must bring help quickly if there is to be any chance of saving her.

Chapter 28

It was a long way to the Skytube station. You know I'm strong, but even with advanced strength, holding onto Al's antennae hour after hour took its toll on the muscles in my fingers, hands, and arms, cramping and threatening to let go long before we reached our destination. But I hung on, finding out early on that the best way to persevere was to keep my mind off my aching body parts, and the best way to do that was to talk to Al. I had many questions for him, and he had many answers, but more than that, Al led me to the answers I needed most without giving them to me directly. You'll see what I mean in a minute, but for now, suffice it to say that the other thing that kept me holding on was something that had been missing in the earlier part of my journey. Hope. The more we spoke, the more feasible my escape became, at least in my mind. To an outside observer, my logic and optimism would likely appear as madness, but listen to what I tell you and make up your own mind.

According to Al, every Skytube station has at least one vessel docked up above for use by humans who meet the criteria. And it's not having a pilot's license that's important because the ships were all run by AI. You simply told the AI the star system and planet you were going to, and it would go to the Pathway entrance, take you to that system and then bring you to the requested planet. Anyone with a Human Purity score of 80 or above and the right amount of money, first, to go up into space using the tube, and second, to pay for the trip to wherever you were going, was eligible to ride the Skytube and use the ships. Of course, this was a big problem. For me.

Number one, my Total Purity score of 59 was a long way from 80. And number two, I didn't know how much money was left on the wristband. It was beginning to look like this was a dead end, but then Al chimed in with a few words of wisdom.

You are not the same man you were when you first arrived here on Aria. Scores can change, especially the Ambition and Ingenuity scores. How badly do you want to get off this planet and bring others to help rescue Gwendolyn?

More than anything I've ever wanted before, I said.

That will influence your Ambition score in a positive direction.

Hope rekindled inside me. *What about Ingenuity? How can I improve that score?*

My guess is that you already have, said Al. *You and Gwen made it all the way to True Eden, didn't you?*

Yes, but that was mostly her.

Mostly, but not entirely, he said. *And she's been gone for a while now. You've been on your own, but you are still alive, still working toward your goal, despite impossible odds.*

And that is because of you," I said.

Not entirely. But let me ask you another question. What else can you do to improve your Purity score?

I thought about the five categories: Physical Beauty, Voice Command, Raw Intelligence, Ambition, and Ingenuity. We'd already covered Ambition and Ingenuity, and Raw Intelligence was what it was. It wasn't going to change. But what about Physical Beauty and Voice Command? What could I do to improve my scores in those categories?

And then it hit me. The hair-cleansing solution! Mada had given it to me so I could disguise myself, but what if I used it to improve my score in the Physical Beauty category? It seemed like a slam dunk.

How far are we from the station? I asked.

One of your hours.

So, Al, I've got this hair-cleansing solution that Mada gave me. Do you know anything about that?

I know it exists, he said. *And I know you will improve your score if you take it.*

Did you know I had it? Were you just leading me down the path so I could figure it out?

I'm not a mind reader like you, Zachary. I only provided counsel on how you needed to think to improve your score. And you have done that. And in so doing, you showed some ingenuity you might not have believed you had. What else can you think of? Time is running short.

Voice Command. Didn't the Teacher say that the Arians loved to sing? I wondered if that was only when they wanted to express their sexual desire for someone, or if it was it more than that. It had to be. I mean, they had a whole category dedicated to Voice Command. Maybe they sang the words instead of just speaking them. What were those words again? *You will obey.* How could I use singing to improve my score when I said those words?

I thought of songs from Earth that conveyed power. For some reason, most of the ones that came to me were religious songs that I remembered from the church choir I was part of as a child. I had always enjoyed singing and was even given solos on certain songs, one in particular. "O Holy Night." I was always overwhelmed with emotion when I sang the first line of the chorus: *Fall on your knees. O hear the angel voices!* It was sung with the tone of both a command and a plea. I would raise my arms into the air, shaking them with fervor, and then I would sing, "FALL ON YOUR KNEES!" Very powerful!

How many syllables were in the words *You will obey*? Four, of course. And how many were in the first sentence of that chorus, *Fall on your knees*? Four. And thus, I knew what I had to do for Voice Command.

I know what to do, Al. Thank you for your guidance.

It is my honor, he said.

I started practicing my singing and wondered if Al could hear. If so, he must have thought I'd completely lost it, finally succumbing to the pressure and going over to the other side of the line that defined craziness. But I had little time, and I was desperate. We were getting close, and Al began to slow down. While I held on to his antenna with my right hand, I reached with my left into my pocket and withdrew the vial, flicking off its lid with my thumb. Without hesitation, I held it to my mouth and drank the nectar. I felt nothing. But then my hair literally began to blow off of my head. My eyelashes came off, and my eyebrows dropped down in front of my face. I felt my pubic hair filling my pants and asked Al to stop for a moment. When he did, I sat up on his head, dangling my legs over the side. I removed the pants and the shirt Mada had given me and held them in the air, shaking them to get the hair off them.

Can you go down into the water slightly, my friend?

Al understood and went down just far enough for my entire body, including my head, to be submerged. I held the clothes above me, and they stayed mostly out of the water and remained relatively dry, but the hair that used to be mine washed away from my body. And rather than experiencing a feeling of loss, my primary emotion at the moment was euphoria because hope not only remained, it dominated by being. I actually believed I was going to make this happen.

Chapter 29

Saying goodbye to Al was one of the more emotional moments of my life. That such an enormous, terrifying creature, so absolutely alien to me, turned out to be not only so wise but so giving, so generous. It was mysterious to me, unfathomable, almost preposterous, but as they say, "He is who he is."

Why have you helped me so much? I asked him.

His answer did not disappoint. *From the moment I first came in contact with you and Gwendolyn, I felt something I have not felt for hundreds of Revs. I felt life! Life the way it is supposed to be lived. A seeking for more. For a better way. Much of that emanated from her, but it is also in you, Zachary, and I feel it growing by the minute. I am not alone in wanting to help you. My people, the Guardians of the seas of Aria, want to help. Because in you and in Gwendolyn, we see hope for ourselves. For our planet.*

I will return with someone so powerful that we can rid this world of those who have oppressed you. She won't kill them because that is not her way, but she will prevail over them. I promise you.

If killing is needed, Zachary, leave it to us. It is, after all, what we do best.

If he could have smiled, I think he would have when he said that. I know I certainly did.

Thank you, my friend, for everything, I said.

We will wait for your return.

Al left me on the shore of a desolate island far down in the south. It was colder here, but it wasn't Antarctica by any means. I was fine and probably would have been so even if it were Antarctica. The weather wasn't my problem. It was that friggin' test and the money! I tread barefoot over the cold and barren terrain that could have been tundra back on Earth, the wind howling and the night persisting, until I reached the Skytube station. The place was deserted. I wondered if there were any humans on the entire island and speculated that the answer was probably no. This must have been some kind of emergency station because it wasn't getting any use on a day-to-day basis. Old Al was more thoughtful than he looked, for sure. He'd set me up as best he could, and now it was up to me to take advantage of his clever ploy.

I entered the station through an automatic door that slid open when I approached and hissed shut behind me, then followed a hallway toward the Testing Center. My heart beat faster as the first moment of truth arrived. Going from a 59 to an 80 was going to require a miracle. But I'd done all that I could. It was time to see what fate had in store for me.

"Please move through the doorway before you to the Testing Center."

A doorway ahead slid open, and I carried on through it into the room containing the pedestals with screens.

"Please approach a testing unit."

I stepped over to a unit and felt the throbbing of the force field as it surrounded me.

"Please look at the screen," came the voice.

I looked at the screen. A light blinked on the screen and covered my entire body.

"Please turn slowly in a circle."

I did as I was asked and, after a few seconds, was facing the screen again.

"Category One score: Sixteen. Yes! A five-point improvement.

"Please begin the next test. Recite these words with your best voice: You will obey."

I took some breaths in and out and really got into the part. After one final breath, I raised my arms into the air and sang with all my might. "Youuuuuu will O Beyyyyyyy!!!"

"Category Two score: Fourteen. Another five-point improvement!

"Please prepare for the next three tests. They will be conducted simultaneously. Close your eyes and hold very still."

I closed my eyes and waited, but I also thought about all I intended to accomplish on this mission and how I would do it. I made myself exude confidence. As before, I didn't feel much, but I felt something. It was like receiving a thought transmission in my mind, but there were no words. Just a subtle tickling of my brain that hadn't been going on before.

"Category Three score: Eighteen." No change in Raw Intelligence. That was to be expected.

"Category Four score: Sixteen." Six more points than before!

"Category Five score: Sixteen." A four-point advance. This was it.

"Total Human Purity score: Eighty. You are approved for Interstellar travel. Please go through the opening and enter the Skytube."

The force field disappeared, a door opened, and I moved through it. In front of me was a kiosk, and beside it was a gate that would either open or not open. I held the wristband in front of the kiosk. Waited. Waited some more. And then the gate opened.

I nearly jumped through the opening, not wanting the machine to change its mind. The Skytube was directly in front of me and opened when I approached it.

I stepped onto the platform, the door closed, and I was propelled toward space.

Chapter 30

The platform came to rest at the station, noticeably smaller than the one where the Teacher had dropped us off. A door opened in the tube, and I entered the station. First, I passed by a single Purity testing unit, then moved into the Decontamination Center, neither of which was needed when heading in this direction. They would be required on the return visit. I could imagine some Arian trying to smuggle in a friend or lover from off-world. If they passed the test, they were in. No passports needed on this planet. Just pass the test. Then again, it didn't seem like there was much demand for smuggling in lovers or whatnot. That was already happening as part of the corrupted system here.

After the Decontamination Center was the docking port for the vessels. Well, I should say vessel because there was only one there, and frankly, it wasn't what I had expected. Small was the operative word. It wasn't even as large as the boat I'd been on that had recently been eaten by an acid-spitting monster from the depths of the Arian seas. I shuddered as I remembered that encounter, and then a warm feeling came over me as I thought of Al. I loved animals, as you know, but that's not the way I thought of Al. He was a friend. A highly intelligent, wise, and loyal friend. It bothered me that the New Arians were controlling his life and the lives of his people. They might not have a passport system on Aria, but they had ironclad control over what went on there.

The ship was shaped like a fat roll of sausage in the supermarket. You know the kind. Jimmy Dean's Pork Sausage or whatever. It was silvery all over on the outside, probably that one-way mirror material that nearly everything was made of, confirmed when I stepped in through the open doorway and experienced a bird's eye view of the galaxy in all directions. The stars were more vivid up here, brighter because there was no atmosphere to obscure the view. Even so, I recognized nothing and was reminded I was an unfathomable distance from home. I took no comfort knowing that this miniature spaceship would somehow transit that vast distance.

There was plenty of headroom since the ship was designed to accommodate beings much taller than I was, and there were two large seats stuffed one behind the other into the tiny vessel, so there was very little room for anything else. There was barely enough floor space to hold a suitcase, but that was of no concern since I had nothing except the shirt on my back and the shorts below it. I sat in the front seat, like a child in a highchair, because my feet didn't even touch the floor. The door closed.

"Destination, please," said the spaceship.

"Sol System. Planet Earth." Now I would find out if I was going anywhere or not.

After a pause of a few seconds, presumably allowing the ship to program the route, the voice came back. "Please buckle your seatbelt."

Funny that seatbelts were still used here in this advanced civilization 580 light years from Earth. But I was more than happy to use mine. If nothing else, it might give me a false sense of security that everything would be okay.

"Point of entry to the Pathway System, Quinta."

I didn't know what Quinta was at the time, but later learned that it was the fourth planet out from the sun of this solar system. The largest of the five, which for some reason was important to the proper functioning of the Pathways, which I speculated must have something to do with gravity. The ship pushed away from the station and smoothly accelerated, and kept on accelerating, and accelerated further until it finally stopped accelerating.

"Cruising speed, point one," said the ship.

I'm no expert in space travel, as you know, but based on the time it took for Aria to disappear behind me, becoming nothing more than another star in the night sky in a matter of seconds, I'd guess that "point one" meant one-tenth the speed of light. This ship was small, but it had some juice.

After around one hour, we arrived at Quinta, looming large in front of us. It was a gas giant, like Jupiter, Saturn, Neptune, and Uranus. Clouds of red, purple, and orange swirled across its gigantic surface, like the colors of a multi-colored popsicle in liquefied form. It had many moons orbiting around it. Wait, some of those weren't moons. They were spherical space stations, like Earth Station, in various phases on completion. They reminded me of the image of the Death Star when it was under construction in one of the Star Wars movies. Drone ships carried supplies to and from the work in progress, and I wondered how many Earth-like planets could be left for settlement in the three galaxies the Arians had been seeding for fifty thousand years.

"Approaching Pathway Entry Point," said the ship.

I saw nothing in front of me except empty space. Wait, was that a gleam, similar to how an invisible energy field would shimmer if the light caught it just right? We plunged into it with a noticeable jolt, and the space around me changed to the lights flashing by so rapidly that my head spun. I became disoriented, nauseous, so I closed my eyes, and things stabilized. I remember experiencing the same symptoms on the way here, so I believe we were at least on the right highway system between the stars.

Time passed; I have no idea how much. But suddenly, we popped into a new solar system like a baby being birthed. I opened my eyes and oriented myself to the new reality. Jupiter floated monstrously in front of us, filling space as the face of Big Ben would fill the field of vision of a man cleaning it.

"Prepare for acceleration to final destination. Earth."

The ship accelerated, but as before, I didn't really feel it, so I'm not sure what I was to prepare for other than knowing I was almost home. I realize Jupiter is a long way from Earth, but in the reality I was operating in, it was a hop, skip, and a jump. We would traverse the nearly 500 million miles between the two planets in seven hours, traveling at one-tenth the speed of light. Along the way, I didn't see much. I thought I glimpsed a few asteroids when we passed through the asteroid belt, and while I very much would have enjoyed seeing Mars, I guess it wasn't in our neighborhood as we passed through its orbital track.

In time, I caught sight of a star that was probably Earth, and as we proceeded further, it became larger and larger and ultimately filled my field of vision with its magnificence. I wish I could describe the emotions swirling inside me when the ship put itself into orbit around the planet I had called home for over fifty years. It felt good.

"Please advise the serial number of the retrieval drone," said the ship.

This was new. "Why do you need that?" I asked.

"I will contact the drone and tell it to execute retrieval and dispatch to the planet's surface."

What was it talking about? But then I remembered Mada telling me that the Arians had drones stationed on all the worlds they had seeded to bring them entertainment feeds from the planet and to capture and retrieve humans with desirable Purity scores. But this was my dilemma. I didn't know any drone serial numbers, and even if I did, I wasn't sure they'd be helpful to me. I was at a loss regarding what to tell the AI. But I had to try something.

"Please contact the nearest drone and tell them to come for retrieval," I said.

"Contact cannot be established with a drone without a serial number."

Hmmm. What now? Was I destined to starve to death, orbiting my home planet after surviving all that I had and making it this far, against all odds? Was Gwen going to be lobotomized at the Zoo on Aria, never to see her friends again and probably not knowing us even if she did? Lots of questions, but as I would learn, in time, there was always one person I could depend on to bail me out of a tough jam. And just as her name crossed my mind, there she was, sitting in the seat behind me.

"Nice hair, dude. I knew you'd end up copying my look. I'm a trendsetter in the area of baldness, you know."

"Maddie!" I bellowed, jumping up and lurching back toward her seat, literally falling into her arms. I embraced her so tightly I wondered if even her herculean body could withstand it.

"I love you too, Zach," she said, chuckling. "Now, turn this baby around! We've got work to do on Aria."

Chapter 31

M addie explained that the Teacher had gotten in touch with her after being informed by the Arians that Gwen and I had been killed out on the ocean after stealing a boat and venturing out into the dangerous waters, without permission and in violation of any number of Arian laws. Maddie was heartbroken but furious and wouldn't allow herself to believe this story could be true. She asked the Teacher to arrange a visit and to take her there, but soon after that, he got in touch with her again, saying that the Monitoring Station on Earth Station had detected a tiny Arian ship approaching Earth. Upon scanning the vessel, it was determined that an Imprint was the sole occupant, and she knew it must be me. When my ship entered Earth orbit, it was simple for her to lock onto my signal, the signal she could detect emanating from all Imprints, and beam herself there.

"The Teacher wanted to come with us," she said. "But I told him it was a waste of his time, especially since he isn't allowed on the planet anyway. By the way, do you think I'll have any trouble passing that test?"

"Not only do I think you'll pass it, Maddie, I think you'll score so high that the Arians won't know what hit them."

"I don't really care about that," she said. "I just want to get down to the planet and find Gwen. You probably know I've already read your mind and know the whole story. These friggin' Arians are a bunch of creepy humans, wouldn't you say?"

"Beyond creepy," I replied. "Darn right dangerous. I hope we get there in time to help Gwen."

I told the ship to return to Aria but clarified that I wanted to go to the Skytube station directly above First Eden. Having accomplished that, I turned and looked at Maddie.

"Jeans and a flannel shirt, eh? Perfect for New Hampshire but not the way to get accepted on Aria."

"I'm not going there to impress them, Zach. I will find Gwen and end their harvesting of the best human minds in the universe for their own selfish ends. And what about that get-up you're wearing? Is that what's in vogue there these days?"

I remembered that I was wearing the garb of the True. Loosely fitting stretchy white swimsuit and a T-shirt of the same material. It was closer to the New Arian attire than what Maddie had on, but it wouldn't win a fashion contest there, by any means. And this made me think about myself. I was supposed to be dead on Aria, devoured by Al, a story Gwen had concocted for him to tell, and he had told it well. But now I was returning to Aria, as who? How were we going to handle that?

"I just transmitted a message to the Teacher," said Maddie. "Told him to tell them I would be accompanied by your twin brother, Ethan. Can you be Ethan for a while, Zach?"

"Sure," I said. "But I think they might be mind readers."

"And you can't block them out?"

"I doubt it."

"Well, that tells me that you and I don't need to discuss the plan."

"What plan?"

"Exactly."

Boy, I could be a dunce at times. "Oh yeah, that plan." I understood that Maddie didn't want to discuss the details, but I knew the Guardians could help us, and she had to ensure we included them in the final solution.

"I've got that, Zach. And the good news is that when I'm reading your thoughts about the Guardians, rather than you conjuring up some terrifying image of a human-killing monster, all I get is the word 'Al.' Do you and Al have some kind of bromance going? Is that it?"

"That's definitely it, Maddie. He's a good guy. A great guy, actually."

"All I'm saying is just keep thinking of him as Al. If they read your mind, they'll have no idea you're actually thinking about a Guardian."

"I can do that," I said, not feeling defensive or looked down upon. Maddie was the real deal, and if anyone in the universe could lead the rescue of Gwen, it was her.

"Good," she said. "Let me take care of the rest of it. Stay quiet and stick with me as long as you can, okay? I don't plan on saving Gwen while losing you."

"Got it. And thank you."

We had hours to kill while we approached Jupiter, so I tried to catch up on how things were going in the Sol system since Gwen and I had left.

"How are the kids and Gino?" I asked. "Are you guys liking my pad in the White Mountains?"

"Love it," she said. "I don't know how I talked you into leaving that place. Heaven on Earth in my book."

I thought about whether or not I had any regrets about leaving, and the answer was obvious. "Leaving was the best thing that ever happened to me." And then a wave of anxiety passed through me. Worry. About Gwen. "We've got to save her, Maddie."

"We will, Zach," she said, reaching up and touching my shoulder. A wave of energy passed into me at her touch. Positive energy.

"Any word from Earth Station on my animals? Are they doing okay?"

"Ye-ah," she said. "They love my mom, and she loves them. The biggest problem you're going to have is getting them back. They still sleep in your cottage, but that's only because there isn't enough room in the cottage where Cynthia and the Teacher live."

"What about Jenny, the older one? How's she doing?"

"Running around like a two-year-old," said Maddie. The Teacher got her all fixed up in the lab, just like you asked him to."

"That's great!" I said. "I can't wait to get back. But I don't want to go back without Gwen."

"We'll get her," said Maddie.

"You realize it won't be easy, right? These people are very advanced, Maddie. They have AI that can do anything, even read minds. And while I haven't seen it, I'm sure they also have military capabilities. At least, their AI does."

"Let's take it one step at a time, okay?" she said.

"Time is something we don't have, Maddie. We need to move quickly when we get there. You understand that, right? Gwen will be processed, and then she'll either be dead or won't be Gwen anymore."

"Message received. Just try to keep up with me, okay?"

"Easier said than done," I said. "But remember, I have powerful friends on Aria. And they are willing to help us. They want change."

"You mean the Guardians, right? The big monsters that you can talk to."

"Yep."

"Well then, why don't you get in touch with them as soon as you can, and let's make a plan with them."

"Just get me close to the water, and they'll come to me."

"Will do."

We entered the Pathway when we got to Jupiter, and I closed my eyes, waiting for the interstellar transport to be over. When we emerged at Quinta, I pointed out the stations being built by the Arians in orbit around Quinta.

"Okay," she said. "They've got some abilities. This might be harder than I had hoped."

"Hey," I said. "If a schmuck like me can do as much as I did when I was there, there's no limit to what you'll be able to do."

"Thanks for the confidence boost," she said. "Sometimes, I forget that I'm a one-person war machine."

We transited to Aria in a few hours and docked at the central station, going through the decontamination process without delay and approaching the terminals in the Testing Center. I was emboldened when I duplicated my previous score of 80, and when Maddie and I came together at the entrance to the Skytube, I asked her what score she had received.

"Ninety-six," she said. "You?"

"Eighty. Let me guess, you scored twenty in every category except Category One, right?"

"That's right," she said. "I got a sixteen in that one."

"That's because you're not tall enough," I said.

"Well, that's a new one," she said. "Normally, I'm too tall for people's expectations about the appropriate height for a woman."

"Not here. You're barely more than a pygmy here."

She laughed, and we stepped onto the Skytube. "The funniest thing is that these beings, supposedly the fathers and mothers of all humans in the universe, have just rated me as one of the most perfect humans in existence, but the people of my home world say I'm not human at all. Ironic, isn't it?"

"Beyond ironic. Ridiculous."

As we descended, I pointed out the dome at the horizon to the east but told her that wasn't where Gwen had been taken. I looked west of First Eden, trying to spot the Zoo where Gwen was, but there was heavy cloud cover, and I couldn't make anything out.

The Skytube platform descended into the House of the One Hundred, and I could see the crowd was as big as before. Ninety-nine would be my guess. I'm sure One would be waiting for us in his private chamber. I turned to see Maddie's expression, and she had a look of astonishment on her face.

"Dang. Those are big humans."

But her surprise didn't end there because the singing erupted when we exited the tube.

Chapter 32

One

Preposterous! That score was invalid. No one had scored 20 on Ambition and Ingenuity since the early days of the Human Purity system. And the highest scores in those categories from an off-worlder were 19 for Ambition and 18 for Ingenuity. It was no coincidence that those were my scores because I'd paid mightily to get them.

I'd been shocked that Gwendolyn Marks had scored as high as me in Ambition and Ingenuity, but now that this "Maddie," last name unknown, had received perfect marks in those categories, it wasn't shock I was experiencing. It was rage. Rage that she had somehow figured out a way to cheat the system. Her total score of 96 would rank her as the second most perfect human in the universe, behind me, and accord her wealth and privileges here on Aria exceeded only by my own. But that wasn't going to happen. I would expose her fraud at the earliest possible moment and have her expelled from the planet. Perhaps I would even have her removed from the human race. I was that angry.

On the other hand, if her scores were accurate, she only needed to get a slightly taller body, and she would overtake my own. She would need only one point because her 97 would trump mine due to the tiebreaking procedures surrounding Ambition and Ingenuity. I couldn't let that happen. Better to subdue her and send her to the Zoo so I could get my hands on those qualities of hers that no one else in a thousand Revs had come close to. Then I would be the Perfect Human!

I watched the viewing screen as the grand entrance of the "Chosen One" unfolded. Literally every single one of the ninety-nine Arians there was singing to her. Every woman and man. I wouldn't be surprised to see a few of them prostrate themselves before her, declaring that the Savior had arrived. After all, everyone knew the same things I knew about the system. Give her a new body and she was the Perfect Human, unseen in the universe since the early days of the Human Purity system, tens of thousands of years ago.

When the pleasantries finally ended, One Hundred brought them to me. The man, Ethan, had obviously gone to the trouble of taking the hair-cleansing solution and scored very well on the test: 80. But what was it about his clothing that seemed familiar to me? I couldn't place it.

Other than that first male imbecile, now dead, the Earthlings were making an impressive debut on Aria. A score of 80 for this man, 82 for Gwendolyn Marks, and 96 for their superstar human entrant, first name Maddie, last name unknown. I could see it now in the entertainment feeds made here on Aria, a new show entitled *Maddie*. One of our famous actresses would be selected, Inez Graves perhaps, to play the mysterious and ever so sexy Maddie from the previously unheralded, primitive planet of Earth. How did she become so perfect? A mystery for the movie to solve, no doubt. But that was wrong, of course. There was no mystery. She had cheated, plain and simple. Gamed the system in ways soon to be discovered by me.

They entered my chamber, escorted by One Hundred. "Welcome to Aria," I said in my smoothest, most endearing voice. I could see the man flinch a little when my words transited the airways and entered his ears, but the woman? No discernable effect. "I am known as One. Please join me for some light snacks and refreshments before we show you to your rooms."

"No, thank you, One," said the arrogant little female. "We're in a hurry, you see."

"To do what, if I might ask?"

"To find the truth about what really happened here," she said.

"The truth, my dear, unfortunate as it may seem, is that your fellow Earthlings are dead. Dead because they ventured into places where humans are not meant to be."

"We know that to be a false statement," she countered. She smiled at me and then glanced at the man, even nodding slightly in his direction as if instructing me to cast my gaze upon him. I did, interested in learning what she had to say about him.

"This man is not truly named Ethan," she said. "His name is Zachary, and you will remember him as one of the two recent visitors. As you can see, while his hair is gone, he is very much alive."

I commanded the AI to analyze the man's DNA and compare it to the previous man, Zachary. Almost instantly, it was confirmed that he was indeed the person the woman had said he was, and then I knew that the Guardian who had dropped off Gwendolyn Marks had lied to me. Perhaps he had failed to capture and devour the man, as is his responsibility for those who trespassed on Aria's oceans. Or maybe there was something else going on. I commanded the AI to read the woman's mind, and it reported back that she had initiated a mind block that was preventing the AI from getting through. I told it to try the man, and it succeeded, reporting that he seemed to be thinking very intently about a friend named Al, whom he'd met here on Aria while boating. Hmmm? All very suspicious if you ask me.

I noticed the woman attempting to read my mind, and she nearly got through until I requested an assist from the AI. This woman was powerful. "How can I help you to find the truth?" I asked.

"Just tell us," she said.

"I have told you what I know, and clearly, I have been misinformed, Maddie. May I call you that?"

"That's what everyone else calls me, so sure, One. And I'm sorry you don't know what happened to our friend, Gwen. Perhaps you can provide us with money so we can retrace her steps as far as we can."

That was an excellent idea. I needed time to figure out what was going on here. Something to do with the Guardians, no doubt, always the biggest worry for any species living on Aria. Even humans.

"That can be arranged," I said. "But of course, I would not advise taking the same boating trip she took. This fellow might have survived, but clearly, she didn't."

"Understood," she said. "We'll leave you then."

"My colleague, One Hundred, will accompany you to ensure your safe transit."

"That won't be necessary," she said.

"Ah, but I'm afraid it will, dear Maddie. We can't have any more accidents involving Earthlings. That would be bad form."

"All right," she said. "Off we go then. I'm sure we'll see you again before we leave."

"I'm sure you will," I said. "One Hundred will show you out."

One Hundred wouldn't stand a chance against this surprisingly powerful woman from Earth, but she would buy me the time I needed to get better prepared. A sacrifice of an aspiring citizen, perhaps, but in the name of Human Purity, it was a sacrifice I was willing to make.

Chapter 33

I led our group of three to the tube station on First Eden, where Gwen and I had begun our ill-fated trip. There were many stations in that city, but I had no trouble retracing our original steps. I was no longer interested in whether the people we encountered were smiling or frowning, so intent was I to make progress toward our final goal. We reached the next island, walked straight across it as we had done the first time, and took the tube in the middle of the three we had to choose from, popping out through the tube as a cork would be shot from a toy gun. We traversed the next island, and I chose the second tube from the left, one of six, and the same one we had arbitrarily chosen since we'd been rejected by the first tube for lack of money on the wristbands to pay for it. Upon reaching the final island, I managed to recreate our wandering path to the automated boat rental store on the north side, where we had managed to secure the boat. I gazed out to sea and saw True Eden in the far distance. That's when things got interesting.

"So this is where you took the boat?" asked Maddie.

"Yes," I said.

"And which direction did you take it?"

I darted my eyes quickly at One Hundred, then brought them back to Maddie, indicating that I shouldn't speak the answer aloud.

Maddie frowned, like a person does when they have to do something they don't want to. "Give me a minute, Zach." Maddie turned to face One Hundred. "What's your real name, One Hundred?" asked Maddie.

"One Hundred is my real name. Our names are not permanent here on Aria. They change every Rev."

"Yes, when you take the annual Purity test, right?"

"Yes."

"You've been doing this for a long time, haven't you, One Hundred."

"For many Iterations," she said.

"An Iteration is the event when your body is recreated, right?"

"Yes," said One Hundred, the skin above her eyes rising in surprise. "You know more than you should, Maddie. Mind reading is frowned upon here."

"That's really not true, One Hundred. You just delegate the task to the AI. I've read that in your mind, among other things."

"You must stop immediately!"

"Okay," said Maddie. "I'm done anyway."

"We should return to First Eden immediately," said One Hundred.

"I don't think so," said Maddie. "I suppose there's no talking you into joining our team, is there One Hundred?"

"What team? What are you up to?"

Maddie turned to me. "Call Al."

I did as she asked, and minutes passed, then the sea rippled in front of us, the wake of Al's approach creating waves as would a submarine rising from the depths. He came all the way into the mouth of the canal, and his head rose up in front of us as he came to a stop.

"Oh no!" screamed One Hundred, turning to run.

Maddie reached out and took her by the wrist, and she nearly fell over as Maddie's iron grip brought her to a halt. One Hundred was over a foot taller than Maddie and probably outweighed her by fifty pounds, but her strength was no match for the superwoman from Earth I called friend. "Stay, One Hundred," she said. "He won't harm you. Unless we tell him too."

"What's going on here?" asked One Hundred, a look of terror on her face as Al rested quietly in the water, ten feet away.

"We're going on a trip," said Maddie.

What happened next had to be explained to me later by Maddie. First, she stunned One Hundred, knocking her out and gently lowering her to the ground. Then she entered her mind and removed all memories of what had happened, beginning with the arrival of Al. At that point, we were free to go.

"Aren't you going to introduce us?" asked Maddie.

I told Al who Maddie was and why she had come, and he actually nodded his head, and then he surprised me. He told me that the Guardians had been waiting for Maddie for a long time. It wasn't a prophecy or anything like that; it was simply logic that someday, the progeny of the New Arians, from one of the outer worlds, would grow more powerful than them and come here to set things right.

My people are ready to fight, he said. *The New Arians have subjugated us for too long. The entire planet has been held captive for too long. Even their own people. Enslaved by a system that is broken.*

I told Maddie what Al had said, and a big smile appeared on her perfectly shaped face. She looked at my friend. "Thank you, Al. Your help is very much appreciated." She turned to me. "Can you ask him if he'll take us to the Zoo where Gwen is being held?"

I did as she asked and watched Al nod once again.

"Tell him we'll make a plan on the way about how to deal with the New Arians. But right now, our priority has to be getting Gwen out of there."

I translated, and Al quickly answered. "He says to hop on."

*****

I did my research before calling a meeting of the Ten. The AI searched the records of all feeds from Earth and culled out information regarding the woman named Maddie. She had been introduced to the world as an "alien" in 2029 by the President of the United States, Gwendolyn Marks. So they were friends. Of course, they were. The feeds showed footage of her disappearing and reappearing, a talent the Makers possessed.

Not long after that, she assassinated the President of a rival nation, someone known as Dimitri Sidorov. Then she disappeared from the feeds. But now, here she was, on my planet. Was her sole purpose here to find her friend? Not likely. She was a known provocateur and obviously not human. She was a Maker spy, sent here to cause trouble.

Perhaps the Makers believed our planet required cleansing in the same way Earth had needed it. But they had sought our approval before interfering with Earth, one of our colonies. So why would they be so secretive about this, Maddie? Why hadn't they sought our approval before cleansing us? There was a lot at stake for them if they invoked our wrath.

The AI was also able to determine the route the man, Zachary, had taken to escape from the planet. A long unused Skytube station far to the south, there to take the One and a guest off the planet in an emergency, unneeded now since the implementation of the revised evacuation protocol, a much more civilized way of leaving the planet. That station should be disassembled, but that wasn't important at the moment. What mattered was that he had no way of reaching that Skytube station without help, and only one species on this planet could provide such transit. The Guardians.

So there it all was. A coup. Instigated and facilitated by the Makers. The beings who weren't supposed to take sides. Who were here in our universe only to observe. Not true. They'd proven that when they interfered with Earth, and while it was impossible to conclude that their interference had produced anything but good for that planet, a coup here on Aria wouldn't be good. Not for me and not for my people. I called an emergency session of the Ten and made my way to the meeting room.

Chapter 34

Riding on Al's head was more difficult for two than one. After all, he had only two antennae. At first, we each took one, but that proved a precarious method, not so much for Maddie as for me. I rolled off a few times, plunging into the water at high speed. I wasn't injured, just embarrassed. But then we devised a more efficient, albeit awkward, method. I lay down on Al's head and reached out with both arms, securing an antenna with each of my hands. Maddie got on top of me and did the same. Trust me, it was anything but pleasurable. Maddie's clothes were soaking wet, and her body was as hard as steel. Her weight made it difficult to breathe and holding on was no cakewalk either.

And while I can conclusively report that there was absolutely no sensual aspect to double-decker ride on Al's head, I will readily admit that I had been attracted to Maddie since the first time I saw her. So what. Everyone was attracted to Maddie. It's just who she was. She had some kind of irresistible aura about her. And I loved her because she had saved me from a life of loneliness and introduced me to Gwen and all the other wonderful people on Earth Station, like Cynthia and the Teacher and Gino, and others. But I loved Gwen more completely, the way one loves a life partner, and I was far more exhilarated by our rapid progress in her direction than by the physical contact with Maddie. Now, enough of that.

We passed by First Eden on our way to the Zoo, which was located on its western side. We weren't so close as to attract attention, but the city was hard to miss, even from a great distance. The skyline looked like a vast battery of missiles that could destroy a civilization. Ironic, of course, since the people who lived there had effectively destroyed the civilization of their own planet. I shook my head.

"What's the matter?" asked Maddie, her face pressed up against mine as she rode on top of me.

"Nothing, really," I said. "I was just thinking of the irony of that city over there. It's a place of great power, but what has that yielded?"

"Madness," she said. "I suppose it happens. But we'll fix it."

"Are you sure about that, Maddie?"

"Not really," she admitted. "But we're in agreement that after we get Gwen, we're going to try, right?"

"Absolutely," I said, determined to be brave and honorable like Maddie was, but my heart knew the truth. I would risk anything for Gwen, but saving people I didn't know was more of a stretch for me. I suppose my life as a hermit in the hills of New Hampshire influenced me in that direction. Regardless, I was sticking with Maddie, for better or for worse.

"Then we better make a plan," she said. "Will you translate my thoughts to Al?"

I did as she asked, and we made the plan. The first part would be finding Gwen and removing her from the Zoo, which would fall primarily upon Maddie, although I insisted on going with her. Afterward, we would take Gwen to a safe place and join the Guardians to execute the next phase. But one thing at a time. First, Gwen.

We arrived at the island where the Zoo was located. It wasn't a large island, but it was fully shrouded by a black dome, like the one I'd seen shimmering in the East during our descent from space, only it wasn't gleaming because night was upon us. The stars were out, however, providing plenty of light for Maddie and me to see. Al dropped us on the beach and slithered back into the ocean. He would wait nearby. Maddie and I approached the dome, which began at the top of the beach.

"How are you going to get through this?" I asked.

Maddie picked up a sea shell and threw it at the dome. A sound like a bug being caught by an electric trap issued

from the spot where it had made contact, but all that remained of the shell was a tiny puff of smoke being carried
away by the wind.

"Hmmm," murmured Maddie. Then she approached
the dome and walked through it.

I knew I couldn't do that, so my immediate reaction
was that she had abandoned me, but then she came back
through and beckoned me toward herself. "Come close
to me," she said, and I knew what was happening. I si-
dled up to Maddie, and she activated her energy field.
"Let's go," she said, and we stepped through the dome.

Inside, it was light. Artificially generated by the dome
itself, probably the same tech used on Earth Station,
which the Arians had built. There were structures in
front of us, only around ten feet tall. They were long and
had pathways running between them, like walkways.
There were rows and rows of them all lined up in perfect symmetry. We walked down one row and quickly ascertained what was going on. The structures were
populated with individual storefronts, each not much
larger than a closet, with floor-to-ceiling glass in front.
Inside each stall was a single human. I've never been to
Amsterdam on Earth, but I've seen pictures and videos
of the Red Light District, where the prostitutes stand
inside stalls like these, displaying their wares. But these
people weren't there voluntarily. As we passed by, some
shrunk back into their cells, while others rushed up,

screaming at us hysterically in languages we couldn't understand, asking us to get them out of there, no doubt.

The people were all shapes and sizes, having been culled from thousands of different worlds. But they had one thing in common: a sign on the outside of their glass that displayed their Human Purity scores, each category listed separately. The scores of the first three categories—Physical Beauty, Voice Command, and Raw Intelligence-were highly variable, but the scores in Ambition and Ingenuity coalesced around a much more narrow range. I saw no score lower than 15 in either of these categories and none higher than 17. I remembered Gwen's scores had been 19 for Ambition and 18 for Ingenuity, higher in both cases than any score here. We searched the entire complex looking for Gwen, and we never saw a score higher than 17. And we never saw Gwen.

"Do you think she's even here?" I asked.

"I'm not sure," said Maddie. "But I don't think they would keep her here if she were. Her scores are too high. My guess is that One is keeping her somewhere else, for himself."

Al had explained to us that the Zoos were filled with humans until about two months before the new Rev. At that point, the New Arians began touring the Zoos and placing bids on various individuals. The bids were placed by category, and the highest bid won. About two weeks before the new Rev, the occupants were processed. The

New Arians had apparently advanced beyond the Essence harvesting tech given to them by the Makers. They could now filter out one category from another, then insert it into the Essence of the winning bidder, removing the old Essence of that category during the insertion process.

"We should find the processing area," said Maddie, and this caused my heart to flutter.

We left the area of human captivity, and it didn't take long to find what we sought. The processing center was just off to the side and was of similar height and construction to the row-by-row stalls we'd just come from. In fact, after the first section, which had solid walls that prevented us from seeing into it, there were more stalls with glass walls. All of them were empty, except one. Gwen sat inside. She saw us and smiled but made no move to get up. Maddie took me by the arm and moved me out of Gwen's field of vision.

"Zach, she's been processed."

"How do you know?"

"I read her mind. She's not the same person as before. She has her memories, but her personality is different. She knows it, but she doesn't seem to care."

The anguish I felt at that moment was hard to describe. I suppose it was like hearing your wife had been in an automobile accident and had lost her memory. I don't know. Maybe it was worse than that.

Maddie shook me out of my nearly unconscious state, whispering harshly. "Zach! Pull yourself together. We need to get her out of here. We'll figure out what to do later. Are you ready?"

I nodded, and Maddie dragged me back to Gwen's stall.

"Gwen, can you hear me?" yelled Maddie.

A nod from Gwen, still smiling.

"Turn around and cover your face. I'm going to break this glass and get you out of there."

Gwen did as she'd been told. Maddie balled her hand in a fist and punched the glass, which shattered into a thousand pieces. I saw some glass shards hit Gwen's back, but no harm seemed to come to her. I rushed into the stall and pulled her around, hugging her tightly. She hugged back. A good sign. I took her by the hand.

"Come with us," I said. "We'll take you away from here."

The three of us rushed out of the compound and back to the black force field of the dome. Maddie urged us to come close to her and broke through the barrier like it wasn't even there. I hailed Al, and he came up on the beach. Gwen smiled at him. She must have remembered his kindness toward us and the help he had provided to her. Another good sign. I sent a message to Al that she had been processed, and he told me he was sorry but that we needed to leave immediately.

We got Gwen onto his head and told her to hold both antennae. Maddie went to the front of one antenna and sat, wrapping her legs around it and pushing her chest against it. She grabbed one of Gwen's arms and held it tightly with both hands. I followed her move using the other antenna, and when I was set, I told Al we were ready. He turned away from the beach and headed out to sea.

"Where is he taking us?" asked Maddie.

"True Eden."

Chapter 35

One

I conveyed my findings to the Ten and was initially met with ambivalence. Two, as always, was my greatest detractor. She lacked one tiny point in her quest to overtake me, but it was an important one. Ambition, where my score of 19 hadn't been equaled in a hundred Revs. And I had already secured a 19 for the next Rev, the donor being Gwendolyn Marks, her Ambition and Ingenuity being held in a trust bearing my name in this very building. I wouldn't have access to it until two of your Earth weeks before the next Rev, but it was mine. I'd made sure of that.

"Why do you insist on calling this woman an alien?" asked Two, always ready to contradict me, no matter the subject.

"Because that is what she is!" I say. "She is a Maker spy, sent here by them to throw our system into turmoil. A system that has served us well for fifty thousand years."

"You have no proof of that, One," she continued. "She is as human as we are, and if they'd wanted a slam dunk, they could have given her a body with the perfect dimensions. She has the beauty, absolutely perfect, and is only lacking the tall stature of our people before becoming the Perfect Human, unseen in tens of thousands of years."

I summoned One Hundred to present further evidence. She stood beside the conference table in the Room of the Ten. "One Hundred, can you tell us where the two humans from Earth have gone?"

"No, I cannot, One."

"Why not?"

"I simply do not know. I have no memory of them after escorting them to the boat rental store on the island of Wix."

"Our AI has confirmed that One Hundred has suffered a memory wipe after being stunned into unconsciousness, I might add. This woman is too powerful to be a human. I can attest to requiring the aid of AI to block her attempt at reading my mind. One Hundred was alone with her without AI assistance so we can conclude that the woman from Earth has acquired the truth from her. If she is able to leave the planet, none of us can know what the Makers might do."

"We all admit to her powers," said Two. "But just because a human from somewhere other than Aria has attained heights we have not yet reached, it doesn't render her a non-human. You know this. Rules are rules, One, after all. And just because her colleague reached the Skytube station in the south, you say it must be a Guardian who took him there. What if he has the same power of teleportation she displayed on the feed from Earth? Have you ever asked the Guardians if they helped him?"

"Of course. They are standing by the claim that they devoured a man who was on the boat with Gwendolyn Marks. But the facts say otherwise. DNA testing proves that he is alive and well."

"Perhaps there was another man. One of us, for example, whom she might have seduced, promising him to couple if he helped her take a ride out on the ocean. It would be worth the risk for her value."

"Malarky," I said, but I was losing this argument.

As if in answer to my prayers, an alert came in from Zoo 1 at that very moment. I told the AI to play the video on the screen. As it played, we saw the woman, Maddie, and the man, Zachary, walking freely down the aisles of the Zoo, then traversing over to the processing area and freeing Gwendolyn Marks from her holding cell. The AI knew something important was transpiring, so it dispatched a drone to follow them to the dome's edge. There it filmed the woman breaking through the force field of the dome. The drone requested an opening in the dome and followed them down to the beach, where a Guardian wound up on the shore and took the three of them away.

"Satisfied now?" I asked.

Two and the rest of the Ten nodded, finally silenced by irrefutable evidence of the treachery underway on our planet, instigated by the Makers and their spy.

"Is the drone still in pursuit?" asked Two.

"Yes," I answered.

"Where are they going?"

"It's too soon to tell, but if they continue on their current course, they'll end up on True Eden."

"Perfect," said Two. "Those primitives have been in our pocket for some time."

"Not all of them," I countered. "There is a bare majority of support for us there."

"So what," said Two. "What can they do to us?"

"It's not them, Two. It's the Guardians. They're in league with these people. Something is going to happen, and it will happen soon."

Two was fully engaged now, as were the rest of the Ten. It was typical for her and me to dominate the proceedings of these meetings. In the end, a vote would be needed, and she commanded a lot of support among the Ten, having served as One for several Revs until I outscored her three Revs ago. I needed her to be on board.

"What do you propose?" she asked.

I used my most powerful voice and gazed directly at Two. "We should issue an Orange Alert," I said. "Clear the people off the streets. Activate the force field and ready the weapons."

Two stared back at me. Silent. Thinking. And then she spoke. "I have no objection to that. Shall we vote?"

The vote was taken, and an Orange Alert was approved and initiated. Hopefully, this would be enough to quell any form of insurrection that presented itself. And if not, we could always fall back to the Final Option if things got out of control.

Chapter 36

Al beached himself on the shore of True Eden. Mada and his village were already waiting for us, having been alerted regarding our pending arrival by Al. We disembarked, and as I approached Mada, I saw him pointing into the sky behind us. I caught sight of something hovering in the distance. It was about the size of a small bird.

"What is that?" I asked.

"A drone," said Mada. "They know you're here."

"What will happen?" I asked.

"They will alert the leaders of villages who opposed you that you're here. They are bought and paid for by the New Arians. They will come for you if you remain."

"We're not staying here, Mada, but we need you to watch after Gwen. Can you hide her and make sure she's safe."

"We can do that. But we need to take care of that drone first."

I heard a sharp sound from the forest. It wasn't like a gunshot. It was more like a projectile being shot from a bow. I saw something that looked like a stone flying through the air. It zeroed in on the drone, which turned to run. But it was too late. The projectile exploded, and the drone was destroyed.

I introduced Maddie to Mada, and the three of us stepped off to the side. Mada's wife went to Gwen and took her by the hand. Gwen made no move to follow us.

"Mada, Gwen has been processed," I whispered.

He lowered his head. "Yes, we know. My wife will care for her. She is a gentle soul."

"Thank you," I said.

"Where will you go from here?" he asked.

"First Eden," I said.

"And the Guardians will go with you?"

"Yes."

"The New Arians have weapons," he said. "Beams of light that kill. And an energy field. It will not be easy."

"Is anything worth having, easy?" I asked.

"Of course not," he said, reaching out and touching my shoulder. "We will protect Gwen and protect our village until you return."

"Thank you, my friend."

"Time to go," said Maddie. "But do you think they could rustle up some clothes like the women are wearing for me? Mine are soaked."

"It will be done," said Mada.

*****

Before we left True Eden, a few noteworthy things happened. One was when I went to say goodbye to Gwen. She was standing with Lalia, Mada's wife, holding hands. She had that placid look on her face that seemed to be the new Gwen, post-processing, and I didn't like it. But I could do nothing about that now except hope that the Makers could figure something out. It wasn't likely we'd get the cooperation of the New Arians, especially since we were about to go to war with them, but the Makers were powerful beings, and I hoped they could bring back the Gwen I knew.

I took Gwen's free hand. "You understand what's happening now, right Gwen?"

"I think so," she said. "You and Maddie are going to go with the Guardians and attack First Eden." No emotion. Just a statement of fact.

"You'll be fine here, and we'll be back soon."

"Okay," she said.

"I love you, Gwen," I said.

She looked me in the eyes. "I know what they did to me, Zach. But they didn't take my memory. I love you too. And Maddie. Good luck to you both."

Yes, Gwen knew what had happened to her, but she certainly wasn't standing up and volunteering to accompany us, which meant this wasn't the Gwen I knew. But I had no more time, so I just had to leave it at that. I kissed her on the cheek. "Back soon," I said, and she nodded as I turned toward the water.

As I approached Maddie and Al, I felt something surge in the water. Then I saw it. Another Guardian was coming up onto the beach. This one was even bigger than Al and had a bunch of scars on its head and the part of its body I could see. I had gathered that if you're friends with one Guardian, you're friends with all of them, so I didn't stop in my tracks, just kept going, standing next to Maddie when I got there.

The message came in from Al, introducing his colleague as Louis and explaining that he was the greatest living warrior of all the Guardians. I'm a writer, so I knew the name Louis meant warrior, but these names were boring. Why not Gideon, or Killian, something that evoked some kind of awe or fear when you heard it? But no. This was Louis. I asked Al if I could call him Lou, and it was no problem. Al and Lou. You can't make this stuff up, I'm telling you. Al told me that Lou would be honored to lead us into battle with the "Pure One" on his head, and I assumed that meant Maddie. I clarified that with Al, and he confirmed, so I asked her, and she nodded. I was also glad to see that Maddie was now wearing the stretchy, dry fast swimming trunks of the True and the top of the same material the women wore. She didn't look like a warrior princess or anything, but at least her clothing properly conveyed what side she was on.

Maddie jumped up onto Lou's head, a leap of fifteen feet, landing lightly, and I wondered why I hadn't thought of that. I had the leaping ability too, maybe not as much as hers, but enough to jump that far, and I cursed myself for not thinking of it before. I had to console myself with the fact that Maddie had a score of 20 on Ingenuity while I had only achieved a 16. The difference between those scores showed up in subtle ways, and I hoped she had some more tricks up her sleeve when the battle commenced. Anyway, I compressed my legs and went for it, made it easily up onto Al's head, laid down, and grabbed his Antennae. Maddie was already down and ready, so off we went. I turned my head back and looked for Gwen, saw her waving, along with the rest of Mada's village. I waved back, then secured my hand back on Al's left Antenna. Maddie hadn't looked back, already focused on the task ahead.

On the way to First Eden, Maddie peppered me with questions she wanted me to ask Al, and I translated back and forth between them. We learned that several thousand Guardians were living on Aria. While there could have been more of them, they had consciously limited their numbers so as not to extinguish other life in the seas and thereby extinguish themselves. Progressive thinking, unlike some humans I knew, known as Earthlings. Nevertheless, I figured thousands of these beasts attacking First Eden would be a slam dunk. But then I learned about the force field the New Arians could deploy around the city, which a Guardian couldn't breach, and the lasers, which had killed many of Al's and Lou's ancestors before the truce ended the war. All of this led to the obvious conclusion. Maddie would be essential if we were going to have any chance of making this assault anything more than a swimming competition from True Eden to First Eden and back.

Maddie told us that she could probably break through the force field and deploy an energy field that would probably block their weapons, but she could only protect herself and Lou. Her idea was for her and Lou to go in, disable as many of the lasers as possible, then open the door for more Guardians to pour into the city. None of us thought several thousand of these beasts could fit in the city, and committing your entire force in the first skirmish wasn't a wise battle plan. On the other hand, she wanted to get enough of them in to tear the place up and to keep tearing until she could exact a surrender from the New Arians. That was the plan, but as you may have noticed, Maddie had thrown in a few "probablies" on matters where "definitely" would have sounded much better.

As we approached the city, I felt the presence of hundreds more Guardians down below, joining us as we drew closer to our destination. All of them except Al and Lou were underwater, and those two had their heads up only to keep Maddie and me from drowning. The Guardians were making fast progress; if I had to estimate their speed, it would be at least one hundred miles per hour. The wind whipped by, and Maddie and I held on for dear life with all of our strength. Well, I held on with all I had while it was probably a piece of cake for her. I didn't want to fall off and impact the water at that speed since it would be like landing on concrete. Ouch.

Soon, the spires of First Eden dominated the skyline and loomed over us like a gigantic army of nuclear missiles, intimidating in ways I hadn't been intimidated before. I saw the shimmering energy shield surrounding the city, and my heart beat faster. Maddie and Lou took the lead, and I got another message from her. *Go back for Gwen and get off this planet if this doesn't work.* I sent back a quick confirmation, and then Maddie and Lou picked up even more speed and crashed into the force field. The sound of a massive thump, like a mallet impacting a bass drum, amplified by a thousand heavy-duty speakers, reverberated in my ears. I'll never forget that sound.

*****

"Two guardians with riders spotted heading toward the city," said Ten. We were still in the Room of the Ten, converted to a war room now that the attack was imminent. Ten would provide commentary while I, assisted by Two, made all the decisions.

"Very well," I said. "Force field strength at maximum, please. They're coming in hot."

The AI made the adjustment.

"How many below the surface?" I asked.

"Around five hundred," said Ten.

"They better not get through, then," I said. "We don't have enough lasers to cope with that many. The energy consumption alone might throw the city into a blackout and cause the energy shield to fail. As a precaution, divert power from the nearby islands to us, in case we need it."

Once again, the AI did as I had commanded.

"The Guardian with the woman named Maddie has gone out ahead," said Ten.

"Yes, I see," I said. After all, we were all watching the same live feed.

"Impact in ten seconds. Nine, eight, seven, six, five four, three, two, one."

I felt it and heard it, even though we were a good distance from the shore, being located in the exact center of the city. Our building actually shook as the sonic blast passed by and rang into our ears as a deep and resounding thrum.

"Did the force field hold?"

"Negative, One. The woman and her Guardian are through. The field has sealed up behind them."

"Fire!!!" I screamed, even though the AI was already firing the lasers with a line of sight at the massive beast and its human rider.

"The lasers are not getting through!" said Ten. "She's deployed an ultra-thick energy field around them. And she's also attacking, destroying lasers in her immediate vicinity with some kind of pulses coming from her own body."

I watched as this apparent superhuman guided the massive serpent slowly up the roadway, helpless to stop them. Could she and this single beast take down our entire city? Wouldn't she run out of energy soon? Yes, she would. Look, she was turning around, retreating, heading back to the sea. But then she stopped, and I heard a burst as the force field buckled in front of her, and more of the Guardians poured into the city. They stayed down at that end, where the lasers had been destroyed, and then I watched their malicious plan unfold. There were maybe a dozen beasts inside the city now, and it had sealed back up as she ended her blast. But each of those twelve slithered toward a building and encircled it, weaving their way around and up, constricting, just as a snake would encircle its prey and crush the life out of it. The buildings began to wobble, and I saw one topple to the side, crashing down onto several others in its path.

How much longer could this woman, who simply couldn't be human, last? But now she had turned around and was coming back up the street, and the plan became apparent. She would fight off the lasers and destroy them, slowly but surely making her way here, followed by the serpents who had only recently been under our thumb. She had given them the one thing they lacked. The ability to resist us.

I felt the touch of Two on my shoulder, and I turned to face her. Her eyes locked onto mine. "The city will be lost unless we act," she said.

"I agree," was my response. "Shall we initiate the Final Option?"

Two nodded, as did the rest of the Ten. A unanimous vote. I gave the command for the Final Option to commence.

*****

I was in the city, on top of Al and fighting, along with a dozen or so other Guardians. Maddie was up ahead, clearing the way for further advances. I marveled at her power, her strength, her endurance. Something was going on with her that I didn't understand, but at the moment, I didn't need to. I would ask if we prevailed, which seemed imminent if her strength held. But for now, there was work to be done. Al and I had toppled one building and were moving toward another when I felt a rumbling. The ground all around me shook, and then I heard it. The roar of massive engines. The buildings nearby literally began to rise into the air, slowly at first, but they would pick up speed soon.

Tell the Guardians to exit the city! came the urgent command from Maddie. *Their force field is down. Retreat! Retreat!!!*

I sent the command out to the Guardians, and Al turned and moved at high speed toward the water, followed by his brothers and sisters. I felt the heat of the flames as the city of First Eden rose inexorably into the air and then the relief of cool water as Al entered the sea and moved away from the massive fireball. I turned back and saw the entire city lifting into the sky. The tremendous force of this exodus caused the Skytube to collapse and fall toward the planet. Most of the Skytube material was deflected off and fell into the sea after contacting the heads of the flying buildings, and the rest was vaporized by the flames before reaching the ground. The fire from the engines was perilous to anything and everything. The flames were concentrated immediately below each building so as not to affect the ascent of adjacent ones, but the heat! It had to be unbearable on the city streets at this point.

I saw Lou barreling down an avenue toward the beach, the last Guardian in the city, and I thought he was going to make it, but then he ground to a halt, succumbing to the insufferable, unimaginable heat. I looked at Maddie, still on his head and at least five hundred yards from the shore. Suddenly she disappeared, reappearing almost instantly beside me, charred but not defeated.

"I can only beam to a location where there's an Imprint," she said, breathing hard and with difficulty. "Thank goodness there's at least one on this shithole of a planet."

We both turned back and watched the city of First Eden disappear into the sky, propelled by a circle of flame, the heat of which could still be felt. The island was a wreck, with fallen buildings near where our attack had taken place and burnt infrastructure everywhere else. I glanced at Maddie and saw she was crying, staring at the remains of Lou, blackened by flames and dead.

"He told me it was the honor of his life to have fought with me," she said, forcing out the words between tears and harsh breaths.

"How did he do that, Maddie? I thought you couldn't communicate with animals."

"I don't know," she blubbered. "But that's what he said. I heard it clear as a bell."

"Where do you think the New Arians are going?" I asked.

She shook her head. "I don't know. But we need to find out and stop them if we can."

*****

We returned to True Eden and celebrated. The potential attack from the villages who had sided with the New Arians hadn't happened. On the contrary, when they heard what was going on, that we were attacking them, they rejoiced, as ready as the people of Mada's village were to cast off their oppressors. And when we returned with the news of our victory, the festivities ramped up even further. Maddie and Gwen enjoyed wine together, although I could tell Maddie was already thinking about how to stop the New Arians.

But there was something else going on with Maddie. Something deep inside manifesting itself on the outside as despondency. She'd just led one of the most significant victories in the history of freedom itself, but she was hurting. And then I knew what it was. The death of innocents on First Eden, likely numbering in the tens of thousands, was weighing on her soul. Look, it had happened, and it was for the greater good, but I write these lines here because you need to know that Maddie is a kind soul. Taking the lives of innocents during the battle was a burden she would bear for the rest of her life.

Before parting with the Guardians, Maddie got an understanding of what they had in mind for Aria now that ten million of its most prominent citizens had departed. The Guardians didn't expect to have any trouble with the people who were left behind, all of whom had been discriminated against for their entire lives by the Human Purity system.

We could use her help, said Al, speaking of Maddie. *And I'd like you to stay longer as well. And your wonderful partner, Gwen.*

"I second that," said Mada. "My people want to help, but we don't know the ways of the modern world. We need the guidance of the Pure One. And our good friends, Zach and Gwen."

I was touched by the comments of my two dear friends and was saddened at the nature of our hasty exit from Aria, which happened after news from the universe reached us, which I'll tell you in a moment.

Maddie promised to send help for the people in the Zoos immediately, and Al took Mada to the nearest "civilized" island to fetch communication gear that Maddie could use to contact the Teacher. She contacted him, and he showed up immediately, telling us that a team of a hundred Imprint volunteers was on the way, using the Pathways. They would help get the humans out of the Zoos and back to their home worlds and help in any other ways they could. There was every indication that the remaining citizens of New Aria would take a new approach based on Democratic principles, and the Makers agreed to help them in any way they could. The Makers had a vested interest in Aria thriving, considering the stations were still needed as their expansion around the universe continued. The Teacher said the Makers could help Gwen get closer to her old self when we returned to Earth Station, which would be soon, I hoped. But then everything changed when the Teacher revealed the destination of the New Arians.

"They're headed to Earth," he said. "We expect them to arrive in less than seven hours."

PART FOUR

Chapter 37

One

"Why are you here?" asked the reporter from the New Zealand station, Agatha Blackstone, who would now become world famous.

"We are here because we were expelled from our own planet by the Makers, the beings who have promised Earth they are your saviors," I said.

I had been prepped and briefed for this interview ad nauseum and was fully prepared to answer any question that might be thrown at me. I had learned English, the most widely spoken language on Earth, and the history of "civilization" on this planet. As much of it as I could stomach. It was always the same with these primitive worlds. The same mundane scratching out of an existence until rudimentary civilization took hold. From the seed my people had planted, I'll remind you. It was a hopelessly boring thing to witness since we'd watched it transpire on tens of thousands of worlds.

And yet, the survival of the Arian race was partly contingent on placating the world on which we now lived. I would make the sacrifice.

"Why would the Makers do such a thing?" she asked.

"The Makers are not what they appear to be, my dear. If they were, we wouldn't be here because they also made promises to my people. All of them broken."

"Why did you choose Earth as your destination?"

Our drone surveys had determined our landing site on Earth not long after the Makers had cleansed this world of all weapons and straightened out their issues with global warming, famine, and clean water, as well as other things like disease, none of which had been an issue for Arians for thousands of years. It was an island off the coast of a country called New Zealand, a very remote place unto itself, with a pleasant climate, a perfectly-sized uninhabited patch of land, known for some reason as "Disappointment Island." I didn't care why it was called that (Ironically, it had something to do with explorers looking for safe harbor, fresh water, wood for cooking, and mundane things like that, none of which they found here. Not an issue for us. We make our own fresh water and cook whatever we choose to cook.)

I answered the woman's monotonous question. A lie, of course. "Because we want to help your people avoid the mistake we made. Trusting the Makers."

"The people of Earth do not all see it that way," said the reporter. "The force field you surrounded our planet with keeps the Makers out, but it also keeps us in. Satellite launches have come to a standstill. The exploration of space is on hold. When can we expect to resume our climb to the stars?"

"Be careful what you wish for," I said. "The stars can be treacherous, which is why we have protected every planet in your solar system in the same way the Earth is protected. And why we patrol your sun with thousands of drones, to keep certain hostile regimes from destroying it, including the Makers."

"We thank you for that, sir, but my question was when. When will we be free to come and go from our planet as we were before you arrived?"

"We can take you wherever you want to go as soon as a formal accord is reached accepting our presence here on Earth. Your own country has already welcomed us and is happily reaping the benefits."

We were already self-sufficient since our fishing drones were out there, providing us with what we needed and giving the surplus to the tiny country of five million people where we had made our home. We further encouraged New Zealand to accept us with open arms by assuring their leaders that they would not be immediately exterminated and protected above all others should the rest of the world fail to fall in line. After all, we were the only people on Earth with weapons of mass destruction, and we would use them if we had to. There were plenty of other places to go in this galaxy alone, should things not work out on Earth.

"When will you travel to meet with leaders of the world? If you want to be accepted, you must reach out. Am I wrong?"

"We are reaching out as we speak," I said. "We invite any world leader who sincerely wants to talk to come here to meet with us. That is our offer. We hope you understand that we fear for our lives in leaving our tiny fortress here. There has been much hostility expressed toward us."

*****

The interview ended, and Maddie switched off the feed that had been beamed to them on Earth Station. I had been watching her as the feed played, and her emotions had ranged from outrage to despair. We hadn't been able to get to Earth before the Arians and probably wouldn't have been able to stop them from landing even if we had been. As it was, Earth had no weapons to even try to fight the Arians with, all of them having been neutralized regularly by the Makers.

The Makers themselves might have been able to stop them, but the Council of Makers hadn't secured the

80% vote needed to take action against the New Arians. Thus the Arians had landed without incident, a fiery ball of light descending from the sky onto a remote island that had obviously been preselected. They had immediately erected the planet-encircling force field, and now nothing could get through, and apparently, that included Maddie. To make matters worse, Maddie's partner in life, Gino, and their two children, Casey and Tony, were down there, and she couldn't get to them.

But I didn't understand why. "You broke through the force field at the dome and the one surrounding First Eden. Why can't you break through this one?"

The Teacher provided the answer. "The planetary force fields are a more potent kind of energy, drawing from the planet's magnetic fields and utilizing the force of gravity itself. The local force fields are the same energy Maddie uses to make her own field. She can draw energy from those and use it to break through. That's not the case with the planetary fields. Even worse news is that the Arians have already figured that out and are now using the planetary field as the energy source for their field around their city."

Not good news but at least that answered my question about how Maddie never ran out of energy while fighting in the streets of First Eden. But it didn't solve our problem. We needed to get to Earth and deal with the New Arians.

"Can anything be done?" I asked.

"We're working on it," said the Teacher, "but it's the same dilemma the Makers had on Aria. We couldn't break through the planetary field and therefore had no idea what was happening down there until you and Gwen made it to the planet's surface."

That comment brought my mind back to my own troubles. We were gathered in the courtyard between the cottages. Myself, Maddie, the Teacher, Cynthia, their friend Jean, and Gwen. Along with my ten animals, of course. The dogs had mauled me when I arrived, and Jack the cat had licked my face with his sticky tongue, forcing himself through the pack while they had me on the ground. It was a joyous reunion, but everything was soured these days by the absence of Gino and the twins and by Gwen's condition.

The Teacher had offered some solutions to us regarding Gwen, none of which were acceptable to her. The most viable option was for the Makers to reboot her mind using the copy of her Essence that is always made during the reinsertion process. Unfortunately, the Teacher said the copies weren't perfect. Something was always missing. Cynthia said it was the divine spark placed in us by God, and she may have been right. The Teacher had no answer, only that Gwen would still be different, not as different as she was now, but not the same either. Plus, she would have no memories of our trip to Aria because the copy was made before we made that trip. Before she and I had met, actually, and that didn't work for her. I was thankful for that. I didn't want to try to get to know her all over again, and she didn't want to risk losing what she felt for me and all we had experienced together.

Maddie believed the components of Gwen's Essence that had been stolen, her Ambition and Ingenuity, were either already incorporated into One's Essence or in storage for later. We all hoped it was the latter. The question was, how to find out? We couldn't even get to Earth.

Chapter 38

One

I will admit that my ego was still stinging from our humbling defeat on Aria. The Guardians are a powerful foe, but they would have been helpless against us without the interference of the woman named Madison Pace. She seemed to cause trouble wherever she went, and I intended to expose her to the world at the appropriate time, just as I had already exposed the Makers. When I was finished, they would all be unwelcome here.

In the meantime, I needed to placate my own people here in New Eden. We had lost over 200,000 citizens during the attack on our city, but that still left 9.8 million for me to deal with. Their issue wasn't trauma from the attack or the relocation here. It was boredom. The live feeds from the outer worlds were being systematically shut down, and I smelled Maker interference. It wouldn't take much for them to gain the cooperation of the nearly one billion Arians that remained on the planet, simply because virtually all of them weren't benefitting from our system the way some of us had, other than the peace it had brought to our world. The order. But the remaining populace of Aria would be easy pickings for the Makers, and there were enough links to the outer worlds left on the planet, especially in the Zoos, for them to assemble a plan for deactivating our harvesting programs throughout our planetary empire.

Meanwhile, with a sparsity of live feeds to choose from, my people here were becoming restless. There was also unrest as to whether or not our Human Purity system could survive with no supply of minds available currently. I believed this was a temporary phenomenon and that Earth had more than enough good minds for our needs. It was one thing to depend on drones to ferret out and secure acceptable candidates on a world, but there was nothing like being there. As soon as we got out and about, our new acquisition methodologies could be deployed, and we would be back in business.

The Zoos would have to be located under the city itself, and the machines were already boring down and reinforcing as they went, and we would soon have an entirely new and exciting city underneath this one. The only potential impediment was Madison Pace. We'd already deployed an energy shield around the city, which she couldn't penetrate, but she was a clever girl. A score of 20 in the Ingenuity category was nothing to be trifled with or discounted. I would need to find her weakness. And exploit it.

*****

"Let's assume brute force won't get the job done this time," said Maddie.

"Meaning we need to outsmart them, somehow," I said.

"Yes," she responded. "Ideas, anyone?"

Maddie, Cynthia, the Teacher, Gwen, Jean, and I were gathered around the table in the center of the courtyard between the cottages. I was drawing a blank so far, and it appeared everyone else was too. Then a voice I didn't know so well spoke up.

"We have to get them to open the field to let us through," said Dr. Jean Lemare.

"You mean voluntarily open it?" I asked.

"Yes," said Jean. "How can we do that?"

Ah, so she was leading us in a direction. She didn't have the answer but was trying to get us to think of one.

"For example," she continued. "What do they do when one of their drones patrolling the sun has a mechanical problem and needs repair? Or simply needs periodic maintenance?"

The Teacher had a partial answer. "In their own solar system, they didn't repair faulty drones or bring them in for normal maintenance. They simply let them die and then sent out more drones from the home planet to replace them."

Now I could make a contribution. "But the drone production site was likely on an island other than First Eden on Aria, wouldn't you think?"

"Undoubtedly," said Maddie. "Meaning we can assume they don't have drone production capability on Earth."

"Yet," said the Teacher. "And they may have an adequate supply for the foreseeable future, so I think this might be a dead-end proposition. I don't believe they would bring a drone back to Earth for repair or maintenance."

Jean's first option had been shot down, but she wasn't finished challenging us to reach further. "What's in space that they might need on Earth in the near future?" asked Jean.

We all sat and thought. I drank from my beer and set it back on the round table.

"Humans," said Maddie.

Hmmm. Where was she going with this? "What kind of humans?" I asked.

"The kind with high Ambition and Ingenuity scores," she responded. "The kind they brought to the Zoos from the outer worlds."

"I think we've all assumed that the Arians will initiate a covert harvesting program on Earth in short order," said the Teacher.

"No doubt," said Maddie. "But not yet. All they have right now are a few measly drones from their old program. They've got ten million people who need to renew their scores every Rev. They might delay that by switching their renewal cycle to every year, which is twice as long as a Rev. Still, it's safe to assume they're going to be running into a deficit situation very quickly."

"If I might add something," said the Teacher. "I'm not sure you're aware of it, but there is a council called the Ten, which are the ten highest ranking people in the Human Purity system, that essentially run everything. Those ten will be looking very intently to hold onto their positions."

Now Cynthia kept the logic moving forward. "So if we could supply the Ten with some humans they could use to at least maintain their scores going forward, this would have some appeal to them." I didn't know Cynthia well, but I knew she was a pioneer here on Earth Station, the first to suggest change, and one of the architects that had built this place into the true paradise it had become. Cynthia was clearly engaged in what was going on here and that was a good sign that something positive would result.

Maddie closed the loop even further. "All we need is an Arian who used a Skytube to escape the planet, absconding with as many high-scoring humans from the Zoos as he could hold on the ship."

"What's the standard size ship up there in the space stations above Aria?" asked Jean.

"A ship for six passengers," said the Teacher.

"Can we get one?" asked Maddie.

"Of course," said the Teacher.

"Now all we need is an Arian and four or five humans from the Zoo, and we're in business," said Maddie.

"There are six of us sitting right here," said Cynthia.

"Which of us will be the Arian?" asked Jean.

I wish I could say that I volunteered, but I didn't. Still, when all eyes turned to me, balder than a newborn baby from the hair-cleansing solution, I knew the role I'd be playing.

Chapter 39

As it turned out, I was the only one who needed a new body to play my part. The Teacher had a body made that was seven and a half feet tall, hairless, massive, and with a gargantuan anatomy. In other words, I looked like One and every other male Arian living in New Eden. My Essence was removed and transferred to the new body, and my old body was placed in storage to await my return.

The others could be changed in appearance with a few minor alterations. For Maddie, it ended up being more than minor because she refused to wear a wig. She had some other alterations I'll describe in a moment. Cynthia and Jean were good as is. We just had to figure out what planets would be a proper fit for them and the Teacher would take care of that.

The Teacher was given a homemade hair-cleansing solution and became bald. He would likely pass the

Human Purity test if we had to take it when we arrived. We had Gwen's hair trimmed back and dyed blond, and she looked completely different. Still beautiful in my eyes, but well disguised. I was worried about bringing Gwen with us because of her condition, but we needed to fill the ship, and it wouldn't be fair to ask anyone else to do it.

The Teacher made sure everyone wore clothes consistent with their planet's garb, which, for me, as the Arian, would be easy but not a comfortable assignment because I was still uneasy wearing see-through clothing. I insisted on wearing underwear until we accomplished something, specifically, getting through the force field around Earth. Jean and Cynthia were wearing brown overalls from an agrarian world named Festiva. The Teacher was posing as a wanna-be Arian from the closest inhabited planet to the Arian system, Trebula.

Maddie, having refused to wear a wig, didn't leave the Teacher with many options for disguising her appearance. He made her a city dweller from the warlike planet named Systyn, and she seemed amused to have her entire body embroidered with tattoos. Real tattoos. The design on her body was a swirling pattern of red, blue, and black, covering all of her, except her face and head, which had a more delicate design. The swirls from her body separated as they approached her throat and neck and thinned further upon reaching her face, sprouting into two delicate sky blue flowers, positioned on her cheeks and ending at the outside of each of her enormous pale blue eyes. The top of her head was the endpoint for a graceful Lily, symbolizing purity and honoring her mother. Her graceful nose, full lips, and forehead remained uncovered, but if you didn't know her, you wouldn't recognize her at all. I should add that they wore very little clothing on Systyn since the tattoos served that purpose, almost like body painting, and the weather was apparently quite tropical. I'm sure you can imagine what she looked like. Frightening and terribly seductive at the same time.

The Teacher had assured her that the tattoos could be removed surgically with no scarring, but Maddie seemed unconcerned. I'm not sure why, but she actually liked the whole warrior from Systyn role and said so. I wondered what was going through her head at that time. Perhaps it was the knowledge that if violence was required when we confronted the Arians, she would be called upon. And by changing her appearance to that of a warrior, maybe Maddie was trying to convince herself it wasn't really her that was violent. It was someone else. On the other hand, she'd already led the attack that had killed thousands on Aria without the disguise, so her logic was confusing. But I'm sure it gave her something she needed. Perhaps the strength to kill again, which despite her great power, was a foreign and highly repulsive act for her.

We were at a loss as to what to do with Gwen, and I took that opportunity to suggest that we leave her on Earth Station.

"I want to go," she said, which was a shock to all of us. Didn't it take Ambition to make a statement like that?

We all looked at each other, and the surprise was apparent among the group.

"Teacher, is there a Human Purity meter on the ship you brought from Aria?" I asked.

"Yes, a portable one."

"Can we test Gwen right now?"

"Of course.

The ship had been brought to our cottages on Neverland after being recieved using the receiving dock at the big warehouse area and the Monitoring Station on World 2A, where all supplies were unloaded. The Teacher had jumped it over to our compound, and it was resting peacefully off to the side of the center courtyard. It was an extra fat package of Jimmy Dean's Pork Sausage, around twenty feet long and ten feet wide, that held six seats in three rows of two. The ship apparently included a portable Human Purity meter, perhaps for Arian travelers to use on those they encountered on their excursions into the cosmos.

The Teacher brought it over and ran the test on Jean. Her scores were as follows:

Physical Beauty—11
Voice Command—17
Raw Intelligence—17
Ambition—3
Ingenuity—2
Total Score—50

The first three scores were the same as what she'd received originally, but the Ambition and Ingenuity had fallen off dramatically. However, they weren't zero.

"Teacher, shouldn't the Ambition and Ingenuity be zero?" I asked.

"I'm sure they were at one point. But we definitely are learning something here."

"It's consistent with my own experience," I said. "My Ambition and Ingenuity scores improved as I was driven to find a way off the planet."

The Teacher nodded. "So there is hope," he said.

I dared not ask him how far back Gwen might build herself over time. How close to her original self she might become. But I was emboldened by her progress, as was everyone else, gauging from the smiles everyone in our group displayed, including Gwen. It was a hopeful moment. Now for the hard part.

Chapter 40

We took the Jimmy Dean vessel back to Jupiter, came as close as we could to the Pathway entrance, and then turned it around. The Teacher had figured out how to make the communication console work, which made me feel somewhat inept since I hadn't even known there was a console in the ship I had stolen during my escape from Aria. But it didn't matter. The Teacher had me sit in front of the camera embedded in the console and told me what to say telepathically.

"Hello, Arians on Earth. I am Arian 10137015. I have escaped the planet and am heading toward Earth to rejoin my fellow citizens. I bring five prized specimens from Zoo 3, which I was visiting when the coup unfolded. These five had the highest Ambition and Ingenuity scores of the entire Zoo. I herded them onto the Skytube and executed an emergency evacuation from the planet. I seek refuge on Earth, but I bring treasure with me. Gifts ranging from 15 to 17 in the key categories. Scores like this are not meant for lowly citizens like myself. Please advise a course of action so I may rejoin my people and help to rebuild what has been lost."

The Teacher explained that the Arians had deployed drones around the planet that would receive the message and transmit it to the Ten on New Eden. He knew this because his team on Earth Station had hacked one of them and been able to receive information, such as the video feed of the interview with One that we had watched earlier. It was only a partial hack, however, and they'd not yet made progress in sending messages in the other direction, back to Earth. Nevertheless, there was no doubt that our message would be passed through since it would greatly interest the Ten. At least, we hoped so.

We waited. The time delay between Jupiter and Earth for messages of this kind was around 45 minutes, so the transmission back and forth would take at least an hour and a half to transpire. However, we were itchy to move forward and saw no harm in initiating our trip to Earth immediately. Since we could only travel at one-tenth of the speed of light, it would take around seven hours to get there. If we were going to hear back from Earth, it would happen well before that.

Two hours after we sent the message, a response came in. "Proceed to Earth. Upon entering Earth orbit, contact Drone 789342 for transfer to New Eden."

Short but sweet, but it was all we needed. We were going to get there. Then came the hard part.

Suddenly, as if she had been thinking about it for hours, Gwen commented. "They have AI that stuns," she said.

"How do you know this?" I asked.

"That's what they did to me," she said. "I'm sure it can be used to kill as well."

All eyes turned to the Teacher. The unasked question was how were those of us who couldn't deploy a force field—Cynthia, Jean, Gwen, and me—going to deal with that? There was no time to undergo procedures that might give us such powers as time was of the essence now. The Ten had taken the bait, and there was no turning back.

Maddie had the answer. "We'll split into two groups. The Teacher will take Cynthia and Jean, and I'll take Zach and Gwen. We'll protect you."

"That sounds a bit cumbersome," I said.

"Trust me," said Maddie. "You will all have a role to play. But you won't be able to stay under our umbrellas the entire time we're there. That's just the way it is."

I wished I hadn't made that comment. But Maddie was right. We all had a role to play. What it would be was yet to be determined, but none of us were backing out.

We entered Earth orbit, and our ship spoke. "Please advise the serial number of the drone that will take you to the planet's surface."

"7-8-9-3-4-2," I said.

"Contact established," said the ship. "Drone rendezvous in seven minutes."

We docked with the drone and transferred over. It was also a six-seater, which made sense. The Arians were an efficient people, even if nothing else admirable could be said about them. We dove toward Earth. I could see the flames of reentry boiling around us, yet the temperature on the interior of the drone remained comfortable and constant.

After completing that maneuver, we were somewhere over the Pacific Ocean, and the drone turned south, presumably toward New Zealand. Within minutes, I caught sight of the great spires of New Eden. (By the way, we didn't know then that First Eden's name had been changed to New Eden, but of course, we found out not long after arriving there, so I am using the new name as I write this discourse.) As we approached, I could see the group of islands off the coast of Auckland, New Zealand, known as the Disappointment Islands. Most were uninhabited, except the largest one, now home to nearly ten million humans from another world. I don't know why, but at that moment, I wondered if the Earth could have stopped them even if it had nuclear weapons and missiles. My guess was no. These were a powerful race of humans. But the powers of the Teacher and Maddie were nothing to trifle with if we could just get them into the city.

The drone leveled off around fifty feet above the water's surface and slowed down precipitously. An opening appeared in the city wall, a new feature that hadn't been there when the city was on Aria. The wall was the same silvery material and was approximately one hundred feet tall. I speculated that it might be a wave barrier since the waves on Earth could get higher than the ones on Aria. I had read somewhere once that a tsunami had hit New Zealand sometime in the recent past. I don't know why I was thinking of such things. Perhaps it's my personality to think of things other than the task at hand, especially when it's risky and has so much at stake. Who knows. My focus returned as we entered the tunnel that led under the city. I was ready to fight to help my planet reclaim its freedom and to help my dear Gwen reclaim herself.

We exited the craft, passed quickly through the Decontamination Center, and entered the Testing Center. The time for craftiness had ended. The time for brute force was upon us. "Please approach a testing unit," said the AI, but we all ignored it.

"Form the groups," said Maddie, taking charge. We formed up. "First one to find the Ten wins!"

The next thing I saw was a blast shattering the door that led out of the Testing Center. We all rushed through the ragged opening. We were moving fast, entering the elevator before the AI defense system shut it down. If it did, we would find another way to ascend.

"I know that One's private residence is at the top of the building," said Maddie. "My group will take him. If he's not there, he'll be with the Ten. You find them, Teacher."

"I'll read someone's mind as soon as we encounter an Arian," he said. "I recommend you do the same."

"Will do," said Maddie.

The Teacher, Cynthia, and Jean exited at the House of the One Hundred lobby.

"Good luck," I said to them. "And Teacher, please see if you can get a reading on where they keep unused Essences stored, okay?"

The Teacher nodded and turned to leave. The doors to the elevator shut, and we shot toward the sky. We disembarked on the top floor. As we approached the entrance to One's private residence, it shattered before us. Maddie's doing. We rushed in and spotted him relaxing in one of the comfortable chairs in his serenely elegant living room. He didn't move as we approached, a subtle smile on his face, and then we saw why he was so relaxed. Gino Morelli sat on the floor, his back up against the wall and holding the twins in his arms, the shimmering wall of an energy shield surrounding them.

Chapter 41

B efore you do anything, Maddie, know that if anything happens to me, the AI has specific instructions regarding them." One tilted his head in the direction of Gino and the twins. "And with regard to this." He held a small vial made from the same silvery material as many things on Aria had been. I didn't have to read his mind to know that Gwen's Ambition and Ingenuity were inside.

"I don't need it," she said. "I'll be fine."

As you probably know by now, my mind can wander at inopportune moments, but when Gwen said that, I felt a surge of pride for her and good fortune for myself that I had met a woman so strong that even at her weakest moment, she still knew who she was and had the courage to say so. Gwen would be okay whether we got that vial or not. I also wondered about all the other millions of humans who had met the same fate as Gwen. It was said that they were all returned to their worlds of origin, and I wondered if they were surrounded by the same friends and family as before that they would regain what had been taken from them by greedy and uncaring people. I hoped so.

The deep, deep voice of One brought me out of my daydreams. "Send a message to the Teacher and tell him to come here with his little group of hangers-on in tow."

Maddie nodded, and the message was sent.

"My, my Maddie, don't you look different. The tattoos of Systyn suit you. But then, you are a beautiful human, no matter your décor."

"How did you find them?" she asked, referring to Gino and the twins.

"Our AI is powerful, my dear, but finding your loved ones wasn't much of a challenge. We simply needed to find someone here on Earth who knows you well. And, of course, Dr. Tom Branch, the Maker representative on Earth, does. He knew exactly where your partner and children were hiding. The old home of our friend, Zachary, here, who seems to have grown in height and stature since I last saw him. Always good to boost those Purity scores, Zach. I commend you. Not that it will do you much good."

"Is Tom Branch okay?" asked Maddie.

"He's fine. Didn't even see the drone that picked his brain."

The Teacher, Cynthia, and Jean entered the room at that moment. I watched Cynthia's hand go to her mouth, a look of concern there, when she saw Gino and the twins. Then I made a point of observing the Teacher, and when I saw him staring at Gino and the twins, there was fury in his eyes that I have never seen before or since. He closed his eyes, and something happened. I felt the walls of the building trembling. The floor beneath my feet shook. There was a ringing sound in the air, like the highest-pitched siren you'd ever heard. And then it all stopped, and silence ruled the room. The force field around Gino had disappeared.

The Teacher turned his head toward One, who now appeared shaken, a look of fear on his face. "No one harms my grandchildren!" screamed the Teacher.

And then I heard the message the Teacher sent to Maddie. *Do to him what I cannot bring myself to do. Please.*

"My pleasure," said Maddie. She turned to One, smiled, and I felt the surge bolt from her body toward One. His fate was the same as that of Dimitri Sidorov. Exploding Head Syndrome, I suppose you could call it. But Maddie was kind enough to keep the gray matter and blood from covering us with gore, surrounding it with an energy field that allowed it to fall to the ground close to the recently deceased One. I looked at the now dead hand holding a vital part of Gwen's Essence and grieved because it had been crushed. The essential ingredients that had made Gwen who she was floated off to nowhere. I looked at her, and she was smiling, not at all concerned about this loss, her confidence already bubbling back to life because she knew now that there was only one way for her to recover. She would have to do it on her own. But she would have help. We already had done so, just by being with her.

Maddie rushed over to Gino and their children and embraced them, her tears raining down onto the floor. The Teacher and Cynthia were holding hands. I took Gwen's hand and walked over to Jean, grasping her hand with my free one.

"Thank you, Jean, for leading us in the right direction."

"We're not done yet," she said. "Numbers Two through Ten are still out there."

*****

I asked Jean to stay with Gwen and sent a message to Maddie to keep them all safe. Then the Teacher, Cynthia, and I left One's former residence to find the Ten. Or should I say the Nine? We found them in their War Room, which the Teacher quickly broke into by exploding the door, as Maddie had done several times already. The AI in the entire building had been disabled when the Teacher did whatever he did when he'd closed his eyes, and I marveled that he was even more potent than Maddie, just more restrained about the whole killing thing.

The nine humans from the group of Ten had fear in their eyes, all standing around the conference table as if they would leave instantly, only if they could. They knew they were defeated and wondered what their fate would be, no doubt. I was surprised when Cynthia took the lead, and then witnessed that she was a power to be reckoned with herself. A charming, persuasive woman. After I listened to her speak, I felt she would have scored very high in Voice Command.

"You may be wondering about One," she said. "I regret to inform you that he is dead. And I am so, so sorry that happened."

"Are you going to kill us as well?" asked a tall woman with a compelling voice.

"Are you Two?" asked Cynthia.

"I am. One, actually, if what you say is true."

Cynthia approached Two, extending her hand. "I am Cynthia Pace," she said. "I'm Maddie's mother."

Two reached out tentatively with fingers nearly twice as long as Cynthia's, wrapping them around the comparatively tiny hand extended as a peace offering. Cynthia's eyes never left their position, pointed directly at Two's.

"We are a peaceful people," said Cynthia. "A complicated mix of humans and Makers and Imprints and reborn humans, which we'll explain in time. But right now, I want to tell you that I believe we can arrange for Earth to remain your home if we can come to an understanding."

"What?" asked Two, skeptical. "That we become your slaves?"

"No," said Cynthia. "We want you to make a decision to become better than you are now. That's what humans do, right?"

Epilogue

Agatha Blackstone, the newly hired anchor for CNN International, asked the question the world wanted answered.

"Why the change of heart?"

The temporary leader of the fledgling democracy, New Eden, formerly known as Two but now known as Rebecca Offling, responded. "At the time of our arrival on Earth, there was an internal crisis of leadership, now resolved."

"What was the problem?" asked Ms. Blackstone.

"As I said, the problem is resolved. New Eden has moved to a new form of government, and thanks to our recent agreement with the country of New Zealand, who graciously ceded control of the Disappointment Island group to our new nation, we can move forward. And I promise the world, you will not be disappointed in what we do here."

"What are your plans?"

"We have applied for membership in the U.N., and if granted such membership, we intend to share our technology with Earth through that body. Control of the energy shield surrounding the planet has already been ceded to the U.N. It appears they will keep it in place, creating openings as vessels come and go from the planet. I think that's wise, considering what is out there."

"Are you still worried about the Makers?" asked Ms. Blackstone.

"Quite the contrary. The propaganda of my predecessor, disparaging the Makers, was entirely false. The Makers are, in fact, the most neutral species in the universe, trending toward benevolence, as evidenced by the help they have provided here and on our former planet, Aria."

"Why don't you return to Aria?" asked the reporter.

"We will if that is what Earth demands. But if I may be honest, this planet is a much more pleasant place to live."

"Why? Is the climate better?"

"Actually, no. The climate is more pleasant and more predictable on Aria. It is the people here on Earth that are more exciting to us. We lost our way for many thousands of years, and now we have a guidebook to help us find our way back to what being human is all about."

*****

The nine of us were barbecuing in the courtyard between the cottages. The Teacher, Cynthia, Maddie, Gino, the twins, Gwen, Jean, and me. My nine dogs and One-eyed Jack were also hanging out. It was the most incredible family reunion I've ever been a part of.

I was back in my original body, but Maddie had kept her tattoos. Gino was okay with it, although he insisted she return to wearing actual clothes. The weather on Earth Station didn't require it, but tradition did. Neither Gino nor Maddie wanted to raise their children to be that free with their bodies. I was thankful for that because it was stressful for me to see the most beautiful woman in the universe strolling around naked, save for the tattoos. Maddie's explanation as to why she was keeping the tattoos was inspiring. She said that they were a reminder, to herself, and hopefully to all of us, of the sacrifices we made to overcome the abuse of power by the Arians, and a reminder never to ever consider such abuses ourselves.

"I love that," said Gwen, as happy as I'd ever seen her. I wondered if she was truly as content as she seemed. The old Gwen certainly wouldn't have been pleased with the prospect of hanging out forever here on Earth Station. But the old Gwen wasn't that far off. We'd been testing Gwen every couple of days using the Human Purity monitor we'd pilfered from the Jimmy Dean spaceship, and she was already up to a 12 on Ambition and a 10 on Ingenuity. It wasn't that we condoned how the Human

Purity scale had been devised or used, but it was the best way for us to get a concrete measure of how close Gwen was to being her old self. She had a ways to go, but it felt like soon we wouldn't even be able to notice a difference.

"I wonder how things are going on Aria?" she asked. Hmmm, that sounded a little too close to the old Gwen.

"Not bad," said the Teacher, who had been traveling back and forth, helping with the return of the humans from the Zoos to their home worlds and offering any advice he could provide. "But they could use some help."

"How so?" asked Gwen.

"In the area of politics," he said. "They simply have no idea how to run a society where a score on a test doesn't dictate status."

"If you think about it," said Jean, an old hand at government herself, "that's what democracy is, at its core. The test is the election, and the result of the election is the score."

"Nicely said," said Gwen, and I very much did not like the direction this was headed. "If they need help, why don't we go there and give it to them?"

I was shaking my head vigorously back and forth when Maddie stunned me.

"I'll go," she said. "If Gino will. And the kids."

"Frankly speaking," said Gino. "I'm bored to tears up there in the mountains. There are only so many hours a day you can hike, you know."

"Actually," I said. "It's the perfect place for a writer, and I very much would like to get back into that."

"Are you saying you want to return to the White Mountains?" asked Gwen, incredulous. "What about the dogs and Jack? They'll live forever, right here on Earth Station."

"And they're not going anywhere," said Cynthia, staring me down with fire in her eyes.

Talk about being boxed in! "Then we can stay here," I said. "No problem. I can go up to Mountain Lake for inspiration and write like mad sitting in the Wine Bar and getting drunk. It'll be great!"

My speech was met with silence from the group.

Gino had an idea. "What say we give it a try, Zach, and if it's not what we want, we come back?"

"Count me in," said Jean. "Earth Station is great, but this is a manufactured planet. I'd love to see a real live new world before I'm done."

I jumped all over that. "But Jean, if you stay here, you won't age, so you won't have to worry about, you know?"

"I'm not immortal, like the rest of you, so I probably won't stay there forever."

"None of you have to," said the Teacher. "And I can arrange to have a station like this one put in orbit around Aria, so the transfer between worlds can be instantaneous, using the portals on the South Poles of the stations."

"Come on, Wild Man," chided Gwen. "You know you want this as much as I do."

Of course, she was right. We had unfinished business on Aria. Friends that we loved and had left in a hurry, chasing after the New Arians to protect our own planet. "Okay. I'll go."

"But the animals are staying here, Zach," said Cynthia, with a firmness I had heard in her voice recently when she was convincing the Ten of what they needed to do next. "I love them, and the children at the school love them."

"Yes," I said. "But I love them too."

I was crying now, over all of it. All that had happened and all that was yet to happen. But the true source of my tears was joy. Joy for my Gwen. She might have been acting, perhaps saying and doing things she thought I would want her to do, but in my heart, I knew she was coming back. Coming back to me, the way I had known her the first time around, urging me on to our next adventure.

*****

Saying goodbye to the dogs and Jack was tough for me, but they seemed fine. They loved it in Neverland more than they had loved the White Mountains. Cynthia took them up to Mountain Lake often, and they could sniff and chase the wild animals up there to their heart's content. They never caught them, but they had fun trying. And I could come back just like taking a bus downtown using the soon-to-be-installed portals between the stations.

We'd all agreed to settle on True Eden and live in Mada's village if he'd have us, which was a no-brainer for him and his people. They held a big celebration in our honor, and we partied late into the night (even though it was daylight). I asked Gwen if she wanted to walk down to the beach, and she readily agreed, knowing what I had on my mind.

We stood barefoot on the sand, holding hands and gazing out at the endless blue water, and then I saw the ripples appear in the distance. Big Al cruised up onto the beach and came really, really close to us, but neither of us moved an inch. He touched his head to mine, and the contact between us brought great emotion into my soul. I continued holding Gwen's hand but leaned into my friend, collapsing onto him. Gwen shuffled around, released my hand, then held her arms in the air and fell flush against him. I stretched my arms up and did the same. Our hands touched again, clasping together, and our bodies draped as one against our magnificent friend.

I am honored that you have returned to help us, he said.

The honor is mine, I said.

Mine too, said Gwen.

Wait a minute. Now you can talk to animals?
Al taught me how. During our long ride over to First Eden.
Another miracle, I said.
And many more to come.

An excerpt from Book Four of the
ANOTHER KIND series:

SONG OF
ANOTHER KIND

Due for release in January of 2024.

Chapter 1

Aria/Earth Year 2046

M addie Pace was uncomfortable as she waited for the performance to begin. It wasn't because she was sitting on the head of a 300-foot serpent named Freya, the widow of the great warrior, Louis, whom Maddie had ridden into battle to free this world from the tyranny of the Human Purity system. No, it wasn't that. Freya's head felt perfectly fine. It was the crowd of admirers below her that bothered her. The ones brave enough to come close to the gathering of Guardians assembled on the beach to watch the opera. The Arians who had anointed her a messiah, arms stretching and straining to reach her from the ground fifteen feet below. They all wanted to touch the Pure One. And Maddie hated it.

"Don't worry," said Gino, sitting beside her and holding her hand. "They'll settle down when the performance begins."

Maddie smiled grudgingly and nodded slowly. "I hope so."

The performance would be the first opera performed on Aria in over ten thousand years. The Arians had always been a musical people, but public performances other than the mating songs had died out after the need to work had been displaced by AI and machines. In short, people were too lazy to practice the art of music other than for purely selfish reasons, such as for the mating songs and the Voice Command category of the Purity test. But a few had continued to hone their musical skills privately, and now they had been brought together for this momentous performance.

The crowd was massive, hundreds of thousands of New Arians and True Arians coming together on the island that had once been called First Eden, now cleared and excavated in the aftermath of the great battle. On top of the ashes, a magnificent stadium had been built. There was an open end to the tremendous U-shaped building, providing a perfect view of the stage from the beach and the ocean beyond. Both sand and water were packed with Guardians, here to enjoy the performance along with the humans. They gathered near the life-size statue of Louis, their greatest warrior, charging up onto the land with a likeness of Maddie on his head. She didn't want to be part of the sculpture, believing Louis should have all the glory based on his ultimate sacrifice, but the Arians had insisted.

Led by Maddie on Louis, closely followed by Zach on Al, the Guardians had fought and won the assault on First Eden that freed the planet from the tyranny of the Human Purity system. Louis had died in the battle. This performance would commemorate the campaign waged for freedom and what lay ahead for the oldest human civilization in the universe, now in the nascent stages of rebuilding itself from the ashes of destruction. Maddie was here, with a handful of other humans from Earth, sitting on the heads of a few of the great serpents, proud to call them friends and unafraid. Most of the Arian humans had lived for generations in fear of the Guardians, but the humans from Earth were not only comfortable with them, they loved them for their courage and wisdom. Maddie hoped that one day soon, all Arians would feel the same.

Maddie and Freya were nestled up beside the magnificent statue of Louis, and on the other side were Gwen and Zach, sitting on the head of Al. Gwen continued to improve and was helping out as a volunteer on one of the islands, in a Community Organizer role. Elections had been held, and one of Gwen's primary functions was to educate the populace on what democracy was, how to vote, and how to accept the results of the election even if a person's candidate didn't win. Gwen's Ambition and Ingenuity scores were still improving, but not to the point where she was ready to pursue elected office. Maddie felt that, in time, she would. Zach was the perfect partner for Gwen, ever patient and always prepared to help her achieve whatever she wanted to try. He worked beside her in a volunteer role as well.

Jean Lemare had lived on Aria for nearly a year, and she loved it there. But unlike the four other Earthlings—Gino, Gwen, Zach, and Maddie—Jean wasn't immortal unless living on Earth Station. At least not yet. She was undergoing immortality treatments so she could return to Aria and live there for as long as it inspired her. The diversity of life there was more significant than any of them had ever imagined, and Jean wanted to study it.

The island of the Homo Erectus held particular interest to her. They were still there, and Jean's preliminary study revealed that they'd always been on Aria. The original speculation was that the Arians had made them using DNA samples, but that wasn't true. The Homo Erectus had been isolated on a tiny island for millions of years and, because of their limited numbers, had remained unchanged over time. It was thought that a group from their tribe had somehow emigrated to the island of True Eden, prospered there, and expanded their numbers to the point where natural selection moved forward, with the first Homo Sapiens in the entire universe being the result. These humans called themselves the True Arians. Jean would return to continue to study Homo Erectus when her treatments were complete, which Maddie expected would be in just a few more years.

The talented Arian, Rederick Cole, called "Red" by those who knew him well, had earned the lead for this performance. Gwen and Zach had found him on the island where they volunteered. Red was technically a New Arian because of where he lived, but he hadn't pursued the goals or followed the customs of the New Arians for many generations. The New Arians were disciples of Human Purity and would use any means, no matter how immoral, to ascend to the highest levels of purity and the power that came with it under their warped system. Not Red.

He was around the same height as Maddie and, while naturally muscular, not overly so. He grudgingly participated in the Human Purity Census every Rev because it was the law, but he never excelled and didn't want to. His scores in the low seventies kept him on the island he called home, the Island of Wix, and the income it produced was enough for him to live comfortably. He spent his days working on his singing voice and memorizing the lines from any number of operas. It was no wonder his score in Voice Command, always a perfect 20, kept his meager scores in Physical Appearance (he was short and had hair) and Raw Intelligence from pulling him down into undesirable territory. His Ambition and Ingenuity were consistently higher than average, probably due to his work ethic and naturally creative mind.

Red had conceived the idea of using opera to bring together the different factions living on Aria—the New Arians, the True Arians, and the Guardians. It was a brilliant idea because song was the one thing all humans on Aria had in common, and the Guardians sang in ways no one had known until the small group of Earthlings spent more time with them, especially Zach and Gwen, who could communicate with them better than the others from Earth.

Finally, the performance began, much to Maddie's relief. Her worshippers were drawn away from her by the music of the orchestra and the voices of the singers. It was beautiful, and while the stage was on the far end of the massive stadium, spectacular vision allowed her and her peers to see everything as if watching with binoculars. Red's magnificent tenor voice could be heard distinctly above all the others, and he more than fulfilled his role as the lead. It was daylight on Aria and would be for another six days until the planet's slow rotation brought them fifteen days of night, but it didn't matter. Better to have light shining on such brilliance than it being shrouded in darkness.

The opera reached its dramatic climax, and Red's voice rang out like bells chiming on Victory Day of a long-fought war. She could tell from the expressions of both New Arians and True Arians in the audience that they were moved. Inspired, she hoped. Inspired to do better. And just as Red held the final note of the final word, for second after second after second, until silence ruled for just an instant, it was followed by a roar from the crowd unheard on Aria for ten thousand years. The roar of peace. The roar of freedom.

Then something changed. Maddie felt it physically and emotionally. It was an abrupt, pulsing movement as if the planet had been nudged, noticeable enough that she nearly tipped from her perch. She instinctively reached for Freya's antennae, as did Gino and the others sitting on top of the great beasts. No one fell or seemed harmed, but something ominous had been set in motion at the very instant the opera concluded. Maddie could feel it. Goosebumps rose on her tattooed skin. A feeling of helplessness crept over her that she hadn't felt so strongly since the bad man had sat in the kitchen with her mom and herself when she was only four. She knew he was terrible, but she couldn't stop him. Now she was likely the most powerful human in the universe, but she could sense that something far more powerful than herself had just grabbed onto the planet Aria. And it wasn't letting go.

Acknowledgments

Thank you to Sabrina Milazzo for her wonderful work on the entirety of the interior of this book and to Damonza for their beautiful cover design.

About the Author

Steven Decker lives and writes in a small town in Connecticut, although he spends a lot of time in other parts of the world, and sometimes those places appear in his books. In addition to writing, he enjoys time with his family and his dogs and taking long walks in the countryside.

Made in the USA
Middletown, DE
15 October 2023

40720463R00186